Dishing the Dirt

Also by M. C. Beaton

The Walkers of Dembley: An Agatha Raisin Mystery

The Potted Gardener: An Agatha Raisin Mystery

The Vicious Vet: An Agatha Raisin Mystery

The Quiche of Death: An Agatha Raisin Mystery

The Skeleton in the Closet

EDWARDIAN MYSTERY SERIES

Our Lady of Pain

Sick of Shadows

Hasty Death

Snobbery with Violence

Dishing the Dirt

An Agatha Raisin Mystery

M. C. BEATON

MINOTAUR BOOKS

NEW YORK

DISHING THE DIRT. Copyright © 2015 by M. C. Beaton. All rights reserved. Printed in the United States of America. For information, address St. Martin's Press, 175 Fifth Avenue, New York, N.Y. 10010.

www.minotaurbooks.com

Library of Congress Cataloging-in-Publication Data

Beaton, M. C.
    Dishing the dirt : an Agatha Raisin mystery / M. C. Beaton.—First edition.
        pages ; cm. —(Agatha Raisin mysteries ; 26)
    ISBN 978-1-250-05742-6 (hardcover)
    ISBN 978-1-4668-6118-3 (e-book)
    1. Raisin, Agatha (Fictitious character)—Fiction.   2. Women private
investigators—England—Cotswold Hills—Fiction.   3. Murder—
Investigation—Fiction.   I. Title.
    PR6053.H4535D57 2015
        823'.914—dc23

                                                                        2015022096

Our books may be purchased in bulk for promotional, educational, or business use. Please contact your local bookseller or the Macmillan Corporate and Premium Sales Department at (800) 221-7945, extension 5442, or by e-mail at Macmillan SpecialMarkets@macmillan.com.

First Edition: September 2015

10 9 8 7 6 5 4 3 2 1

*To Martin Palmer with many thanks
for all his hard work*

Dishing the Dirt

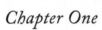

Chapter One

After a dismal grey winter, spring came to the village of Carsely in the Cotswolds, bringing blossoms, blue skies and warm breezes.

But somewhere, in the heart of one private detective, Agatha Raisin, storms were brewing.

When Agatha had been a member of the now defunct Ladies Society, she had got to know all the incomers to the village. But as most of her time was taken up away from the village, she did not recognise the thin woman who hailed her one Sunday when she was putting out the trash, ready for collection.

"It is Mrs. Raisin, is it not?" she called out in a reedy voice.

Agatha came to the fence of her thatched cottage. "I am Victoria Bannister," said the woman. "I do so admire you."

Victoria was somewhere in her eighties with a long face and a long thin nose and large pale eyes.

"Oh, I just do my job," said Agatha.

"But you have come such a long way from your poor beginnings," said Victoria.

"What poor beginnings?" snarled Agatha. She had been brought up in a Birmingham slum and somehow always dreaded that somewhere, someone would penetrate her lacquer of sophistication and posh accent.

"I heard you came from such a bad start with drunken parents. I do so admire you," Victoria said again, her pale eyes scrutinising Agatha's face.

"Piss off!" said Agatha furiously and went into her cottage and slammed the door.

Victoria walked off down Lilac Lane feeling happy. She enjoyed goading people.

Inside her cottage, Agatha stared bleakly at her reflection in the hall mirror. She had glossy brown hair and small bearlike eyes, a generous mouth, and although quite small in stature, had long well-shaped legs. Over the years, she had laminated herself with the right clothes, and the right accent. But deep down, she felt vulnerable. She was in her early fifties, which she reminded herself daily was now considered today's forties.

She knew her ex-husband, James Lacey, a travel writer, had just returned from abroad. He was aware of her background as was her friend, Sir Charles Fraith. Surely neither of them would have gossiped. She had challenged James before and he had denied it. But she had to be sure. That therapist, Jill Davent, who had moved to the village had somehow known of her background. James had sworn then he had never told her anything, but how else would the woman have known?

Agatha had visited Jill, prompted by jealousy because James had been seen squiring her around. She had told Jill a highly romanticised story of her youth, but Agatha had left in a fury when Jill accused her of lying.

"Any odd and sod can call themselves a therapist these days," she said to her cats. "Charlatans, the lot of them!"

She went next door to his cottage and rang the bell. James answered and smiled in welcome. "Come in, Agatha. I've got coffee ready. If you must smoke, we'll have it in the garden."

Agatha agreed to go into the garden, not because she particularly wanted to smoke, but because the inside of James's cottage with its bachelor surroundings always reminded her how little impact she had made on his life when they were married.

Blackbirds pecked at the shabby lawn. A magnolia tree at the bottom of the garden was about to burst into bloom, raising pink buds up to the pale blue sky.

James came out with two mugs of coffee and an ashtray.

"Someone's been gossiping about me," said Agatha. "It must be Jill Davent. Someone's found out about my background."

"I could never understand why you are so ashamed of your upbringing," said James. "What does it matter?"

"It matters to me," said Agatha. "The Gloucestershire middle classes are very snobby."

"Only the ones not worth knowing," said James.

"Like some of your friends? Did you tell anyone?"

"Of course not. I told you before. I do not discuss you with anyone."

But Agatha saw a little flash of uneasiness in his blue eyes. "You did say something about me and recently, too."

He ran his fingers through his thick black hair, hair that only showed a little grey at the temples. He cursed Agatha's intuition.

"I didn't say anything about your background but I took Jill out for dinner and she asked a lot of questions about you, but I only talked about your cases."

"She's counselling Gwen Simple. She knows I was on that case where I nearly ended up in one of her son's meat pies."

Agatha's last case had concerned a Sweeny Todd of a murderer over at Winter Parva. Although she suspected his mother, Gwen, of having helped in the murders, no proof was found against the woman.

"Actually, it was more or less on your behalf that I took not only Jill out for dinner, but Gwen as well."

Agatha stared at him, noticing that James with his tall, athletic body was as handsome as ever. Jill looked like a constipated otter, but there was something about Gwen Simple that made men go weak at the knees.

"So what did creepy, slimy Gwen have to say for herself?" she asked.

"Agatha! The poor woman is still very traumatised. Jill did most of the talking."

Gwen probably sat there with a mediaeval-type gown on to suit her mediaeval-type features, thought Agatha bitterly. That one doesn't even have to open her mouth. She just sits there and draws men in.

"So did Jill have anything to say about the case?" she asked. "And I thought Gwen had sold the bakery and moved."

"Jill naturally will not tell me what a client says," remarked James. "And Gwen has moved to Ancombe."

"I would have thought she would want to get as far away from Winter Parva as possible," said Agatha. "I mean, a lot of the villagers must think she's guilty."

"On the contrary, they have been most sympathetic."

"Tcha!" said Agatha Raisin.

Agatha decided to call on her friend, Mrs. Bloxby. She suddenly wondered why on earth this therapist should have gone to such lengths as to ferret out her background. As usual, the vicar's wife was pleased to see her although, as usual, her husband was not. He slammed into his study.

As Mrs. Bloxby led the way into the garden, Agatha poured out her worries. "I'll get you a glass of sherry," said Mrs. Bloxby soothingly.

As she waited for her friend to come back, Agatha felt herself beginning to relax. Over in the churchyard, daffodils were swaying in the breeze amongst the old gravestones. In front of her, a blackbird pecked for worms on the lawn.

Mrs. Bloxby returned with a decanter of sherry and two glasses. After she had finished pouring out the drinks, she said, "I find it most odd that Miss Davent should obviously have gone to such lengths to dig up your background. She must see you as a threat. And if she sees you as a threat, what has she got to hide?"

"I should have thought of that," said Agatha. "I'm slipping. And why bring her business to Carsely? Surely she would get more clients in town."

"I think she *makes* clients," said the vicar's wife.

"What do you mean?"

"For example, she called on me. She said it must be awful for me not to have had any children. That, you see, is a vulnerable spot. She was trying to draw me in so that I would decide to use her services. I told her I was very busy and showed her the door. Everyone has some weakness, some frailty. I do not want to spread gossip, but she has built up quite a client base. They come from villages round about as well as here. She is a very clever woman. You have been so outraged about her finding out about your background that you did not stop to wonder why she had targeted you in this way."

On Monday morning, Agatha's small staff gathered for a briefing. There was Toni Gilmour, blond, young and beautiful; Simon Black with his jester's face; ex-policeman Patrick Mulligan; Phil Marshall, gentle and white-haired; and her secretary, Mrs. Freedman.

Agatha had decided she had given up caring about her lousy background and so she told them that somehow

Jill had gone out to target her and she wondered why. "We've got other work to do," she said, "but if you have any spare time, see what you can find out about her. Anyone these days can claim to be a therapist without qualifications. I can't remember if she had any sort of certificates on her walls."

"Why don't I just visit her and ask her why she is targeting you?" said Phil. "She'll deny it, but I could have a look around."

"Good idea," said Agatha.

"I'll phone now and see if I can get an appointment for this evening," said Phil.

"You'd better take sixty pounds with you," said Agatha. "I'm sure that one will look on any visit as a consultation."

Phil made his way to Jill's cottage that evening, having secured an appointment for eight o'clock. The cottage was on the road leading out of Carsely. It had formerly been an agricultural labourer's cottage and was built of red brick, two storied, and rather dingy looking. Phil, who lived in Carsely, knew it had lain empty for some time. There was a small, unkempt garden in the front with a square of mossy grass and two laurel bushes.

The curtains were drawn but he could see that lights were on in the house. He rang the bell and waited.

Jill answered the door and looked him up and down from his mild face and white hair to his highly polished shoes.

"Come in," she said. There was a dark little hall. She opened a door to the left of it and ushered him into her consulting room. Phil looked at the walls. He noticed there were several framed diplomas. The walls were painted dark green and the floor was covered in a dark green carpet. The room had a mahogany desk which held a Victorian crystal inkwell, a phone and nothing else on its gleaming surface. There was a comfortable leather chair facing her and a standard lamp with a fringed shade in one corner, shedding a soft light.

Jill sat behind her desk and waved a hand to indicate he should take the seat opposite.

"How can I help you?" she asked. She had a deep, husky voice.

"I work for Agatha Raisin," said Phil, "and it is well known in the village that you have been spreading tales about her poor upbringing. Why?"

"Because she wasted my time. Any more questions?"

"You are supposed to help people," said Phil in his gentle voice. "You are not supposed to go around trying to wreck their reputation. Your behaviour was not that of a caring therapist."

"Get the hell out of here!" screamed Jill with sudden and startling violence.

Phil rose to his feet, clutched his heart, grabbed the desk for support, and then collapsed on the floor.

"Stupid old fart," said Jill. "Too damn old for the job. I'd better get an ambulance." She picked up the phone from her desk and left the room.

Phil got quickly to his feet, took out a miniature camera and photographed the certificates on the wall before sinking back down to the floor and closing his eyes.

She returned and stared down at him. "With any luck, you're dead," she said viciously, and then left the room again. She had not even bothered to search for a pulse or even loosen his collar.

Phil got to his feet again and moved quietly into the hall. He could hear Jill's voice in the other room, but could not make out what she was saying.

He opened the front door and walked back down the hill. He would print the photos and e-mail them to Agatha's computer.

Later that evening, Agatha decided to walk up to the local pub for a drink. As she left, she saw James welcoming Jill and felt a sour stab of jealousy.

In a corner of the pub were three blond women the locals had dubbed "the trophy wives." They were each married to rich men and were rumoured to be third or even fourth wives. They were left in the country during the week, each looking as if she were pining for London. They were remarkably alike with their trout-pout mouths, salon tans, expensive clothes and figures maintained by strict diet and personal trainers.

Do women have trophy husbands? wondered Agatha. Perhaps, she thought ruefully, that now she had no longings for James, she wanted him to be kept single so that she could bask in his handsome company, a sort of "see what I've got" type of thing.

The pub door opened and Sir Charles Fraith strolled in, tailored and barbered, and almost catlike with his smooth blond hair and neat features. He saw Agatha, got a drink from the bar and went to join her.

"How's things?" he asked.

"Awful." Agatha told him all about Jill Davent.

"So she sees you as a threat," said Charles. "What's she got to be scared of?"

"That's what I'm trying to find out," said Agatha. "I'm furious. Phil went there this evening and got some pics of her certificates. He's sending them over."

"I bet you've been playing into her hands by raging all over the place," said Charles. "You're an old-fashioned snob, Aggie. This is an age when people who have risen from unfortunate beginnings brag about it all over the place."

"I am not a snob," howled Agatha, and the trophy wives giggled.

"Oh, don't laugh too hard," snarled Agatha. "Your Botox is cracking."

"You're a walking embarrassment," said Charles. "Let's get back to your computer and look at those pictures."

Agatha saw Charles's travel bag parked in her hall and scowled. She often resented the way he walked in and out of her life, and sometimes, on rare occasions, in and out of her bed.

They both sat in front of the computer. "Here we are," said Agatha. "Good old Phil. Let's see. An MA from the University of Maliumba. Where's that?"

"Africa. You can pay up and get a degree in anything. It was on the Internet at one time."

"A diploma in aromatherapy from Alternative Health in Bristol. A diploma in tai chi."

"Where's that from?"

"Taiwan."

"The woman's a phony, Agatha. Forget her."

"I can't, Charles. She's counselling Gwen Simple and I swear that woman helped in those murders. I'd like to see her records."

"Oh, let's forget the dratted woman," said Charles, stifling a yawn. "I'm going to bed. Coming?"

"Later. And to my *own* bed."

Agatha would not admit that she was sometimes lonely, but she felt a little pang when Charles announced breezily at breakfast that he was going home.

For the rest of the week, she and her staff were very busy and had to forget about Jill.

But by the week-end, what the locals called "blackthorn winter" arrived, bringing squally showers of rain and sleet.

Agatha decided to motor to Oxford and treat herself to a decent lunch. Her cats, Boswell and Hodge, twisted around her ankles, and she wished she could take them with her.

She parked in Gloucester Green car park, wincing at the steep price and began to walk up to Cornmarket. This was Oxford's main shopping street and one ignored in the Morse series, the producers correctly guessing that viewers wanted dreaming spires and colleges and not crowds of shoppers and chain stores.

Agatha had initially planned to treat herself to lunch at the Randolph Hotel, but instead she walked into Mc-Donald's, ignoring the cry from a wild-eyed woman of, "Capitalist swine." Agatha ordered a burger, fries and a black coffee and secured a table by looming over two students and driving them away. She wished she had gone to the Randolph instead. It was all the fault of the politically correct and people like that woman who had shouted at her, she reflected. It was the sort of thing that made you want to buy a mink coat, smoke twenty a day and eat in McDonald's out of sheer bloody-mindedness.

She became aware that she was being studied by a small, grey-haired man on the other side of the restaurant. When he saw Agatha looking at him, he gave a half smile and raised a hand in greeting.

Agatha finished her meal, and, on her road out, stopped at his table. "Do I know you?" she asked.

"No, but we're in the same profession," he said. "I'm Clive Tremund. I'd like to compare notes. Would you like to get out of here and go for a drink? What about the Randolph? I could do with a bit of posh."

Along Cornmarket, he talked about how he had recently moved to Oxford from Bristol to set up his agency.

In the bar of the Randolph, Agatha, who had taken note of his cheap suit, said, "I'll get the drinks."

"I'll be able to get you on my expenses," he said.

Agatha waited until the waiter had taken their order and come back with their drinks, and asked him what he had meant. "Never tell me I am one of your cases!"

"The only reason I am breaking the confidentiality of a client," said Clive, "is because the bitch hasn't paid anything so far and it looks as if she isn't going to."

"Would that bitch be a therapist called Jill Davent?"

"The same. I was supposed to ferret out everything I could about you. Got your birth certificate and took it from there."

"I'll kill her! Did she give a reason?"

"She said she was about to be married to a James Lacey, your ex. Said if you had got him to marry you, she might learn something by knowing all about you."

"I think it's because she's hiding something and wants to keep me away," said Agatha.

"Don't tell her I told you," said Clive. "She may yet pay me, although I'll probably have to take her to the Small Claims Court. She was one of my first clients."

"Why did you leave Bristol?"

"Got a divorce. Didn't want to see her with her new bloke. It hurts. Then I had to get my private detective's licence."

"I've just got one of those," said Agatha. "How's business?"

"Picking up. Missing students, students on drugs, anxious parents, that sort of thing."

"What did you make of the Davent woman?"

"She seemed pretty straightforward, until I gave her the report on you, and then she was sort of gleeful in a spiteful way. I asked for my fee and she demanded more. She told me your first husband had been murdered and maybe the police had got it wrong and you did it yourself. I haven't done anything about it. I sent her an e-mail, saying until she paid something, I couldn't go on. She had an office in Mircester before she moved to Carsely."

"I'll pay you instead," said Agatha. "Send me a written statement about the reasons she gave for employing you." Agatha took out her cheque book. "I will pay you now." She scribbled a cheque and handed it over.

"This is generous," said Clive. "I'll be glad not to see her again, except maybe in court. She gave me the creeps."

As Agatha drove back to Carsely, she could feel her anger mounting. As she turned down into the road leading to the village and to Jill's cottage, an elderly Ford was driving in the middle of the road. She honked her horn furiously, but the car in front continued on in the middle of the road at twenty miles an hour.

Victoria Bannister was the driver. She finally saw Agatha pull up outside Jill's cottage, and stopped as well a little way down the road. Her long nose twitching with curiosity, Victoria decided to see if she could hear what Agatha was up to.

The window of Jill's consulting room was open and Agatha's voice sounded out, loud and clear.

"How dare you hire a detective to probe into my life. Leave me alone or I'll kill you. But before I murder you, you useless piece of garbage, I am going to sue you for intrusion of privacy."

Said Jill, "And that will be a joke coming from a woman who earns her money doing just that."

Agatha stormed out as Victoria scampered down the road to her car and this time, drove off at sixty miles an hour.

Chapter Two

Mrs. Bloxby had been worried ever since Agatha had told her all about Jill having paid a private detective to look into her background. The vicar's wife felt that Mrs. Raisin should simply have asked Miss Davent *why* she had gone to such lengths.

Two days after Agatha's confrontation with the therapist was clear and quite cold. The waxy blossoms of the magnolia tree in the vicarage garden shone against the night sky where that peculiar blue moon was rising, a blue moon everyone had been told was because of forest fire in Canada.

Mrs. Bloxby came to a sudden decision. She would visit this therapist and ask her herself.

Mrs. Bloxby put on her old serviceable tweed coat and set out to walk through the village and up the hill to Jill's cottage.

She rang the bell and waited. A light was on in the consulting room. Perhaps, thought Mrs. Bloxby, a consultation was in progress and the therapist had decided not to answer the door. But having come this far, she was reluctant to leave. She banged on the door and shouted, "Anyone there!"

Silence.

Mrs. Bloxby walked to the window of the consulting room and peered through a gap in the curtains. She let out a startled gasp. She could see a pair of feet on the floor but the rest was masked by a desk.

She went back to the door and tried the handle. The door was unlocked.

Mrs. Bloxby went straight to the consulting room and walked round the desk. The ghastly distorted face of Jill Davent stared up at her. A coloured scarf had been wound tightly round her neck.

The vicar's wife backed slowly away, as if before royalty. Her legs felt weak and she was beginning to tremble.

She made it outside and, fishing in her old battered

leather handbag, took out her mobile phone and dialled 999.

It seemed to take ages for the police to arrive and as she stood there the pitiless blue moon rose higher in the sky.

Mrs. Bloxby let out a gulp of relief when she at last heard the approaching sirens.

It was only when she was back at the vicarage, having given her preliminary statement and been hugged by her worried husband, that she realised she should really phone Agatha Raisin.

Agatha was on her road home when Mrs. Bloxby phoned. Her first reaction was, "Oh, God! I threatened to kill her!"

"Did anyone hear you?" asked Mrs. Bloxby.

"No. I bet it was Gwen Simple. I swear that woman's a murderer."

As Agatha drove down into the village, she could see the police cars and ambulance and a little knot of villagers standing behind the police tape.

Her friend, Detective Sergeant Bill Wong, and Inspector Wilkes could be seen waiting outside the cottage for the forensic team to do their work. Agatha parked her car up the road and walked forward to join the crowd.

Victoria Bannister saw her approach and called out loudly, "There's the murderer. I heard her threatening to kill her."

Wilkes swung round, saw the contorted accusing face of Victoria and that she was pointing at Agatha.

"Wong," he said to Bill, "get that Raisin woman here and whoever that woman is who's accusing her."

How many weary hours have I spent in this interviewing room, having questions fired at me? thought Agatha dismally. She had been taken to police headquarters and Wilkes was interrogating her.

Over and over again, Agatha explained that she had found out that Jill had hired a private detective to ferret into her background and that had enraged her.

"I like my unfortunate upbringing to be kept quiet," she explained.

"You're a snob," said Wilkes nastily. "My father was a porter on the railroad and my mother worked in a factory. I'm proud of them."

"I am sure they were sterling people," said Agatha wearily, "but did *they* force you to work in a factory and then take your wages to buy booze? And did it ever cross your mind that she wanted to get me off her case? She was counselling Gwen Simple, for a start. And why did she leave Mircester?"

"That's for us to find out and for you to keep your nose out of police business," snapped Wilkes.

Agatha explained she had not left the office until eight o'clock in the evening. She had stopped for petrol outside Mircester. Yes, she had the receipt.

Agatha looked to Bill for sympathy but his face was blank.

By the time she was allowed to go and told not to leave the country, Agatha was in a rage.

Mrs. Bloxby, who had driven her to police headquarters, got the full blast of Agatha's tirade on the road back to Carsely. At last, when Agatha had paused for breath, Mrs. Bloxby said mildly, "But what a great incentive to find out who murdered her. I am sure it would be a wonderful idea to get revenge on Mr. Wilkes."

"Yes," said Agatha slowly. "There must be something fishy in Jill's background. I've asked that private detective of hers to detect for me."

Mrs. Bloxby looked surprised. "Why did you do that? You have detectives of your own."

"True," said Agatha. "I did it on the spur of the minute, but I will need all the help I can get. You see, there suddenly seems to be a great amount of adultery going on, and much as I hate divorce cases, they pay well and we are all stretched to the limit. Now I know you don't like to gossip, but I have to start somewhere. Who in Carsely has been consulting Jill?"

"I suppose there's no harm in telling you. There is your cleaner, Mrs. Simpson."

"What! Doris? She's the sanest person I know. Anyone else?"

"I believe Miss Bannister went to see her."

"That old cow. I could murder *her*."

"Mrs. Raisin!"

"Well, she's the reason I have been stuck in the police station half the night. Who else?"

"Old Mrs. Tweedy."

"You mean the old girl who lives round the corner from the vicarage. What's up with her?"

"Nothing more than loneliness, I should think," said Mrs. Bloxby. Then she added reluctantly, "Mr. Lacey spent a great deal of time with Miss Davent. Of course, there were women from the other villages but I don't know who they are."

As Mrs. Bloxby turned the corner into Lilac Lane where Agatha lived, they saw a car parked outside James's cottage. Bill Wong and detective Alice Peterson were just getting out of it. Bill saw Agatha and signalled to the vicar's wife to stop. "Don't go to bed yet," he said to Agatha. "I want to ask you a few more questions. Mrs. Bloxby, a minute of your time."

"Do you want me to come in with you?" asked Mrs. Bloxby as Agatha got out of the car at her cottage.

"No, you've done enough and thank you," said

Agatha. She had a sudden impulse to hug Mrs. Bloxby, but resisted. Agatha Raisin, somehow, could not hug anyone—handsome men excepted.

Once inside her cottage, she slumped down on her sofa. The cats prowled around her hopefully. Agatha often forgot that she had fed them and would feed them again, but this time, she felt too tired to move.

Her eyes were just closing when she heard the imperative summons of her doorbell. She struggled to her feet, went to open it and stared bleakly at the two detectives.

Agatha led the way to the kitchen. "Have a seat and make it quick," she said.

"We've got to go over it again," said Bill soothingly. "You should know better than to go around threatening to kill people."

"I was exasperated," said Agatha. "How dare she hire a private detective to dig up my background?"

"We will be interviewing Clive Tremund," said Bill. "Begin at the beginning."

Agatha did not want to say again that she had initially lied to Jill about her upbringing. Tell a detective that you've lied about one thing and they might assume you're lying about everything else. She detailed the previous day. She had been working on a divorce case and had been out on it with Phil. He had the pictures to prove it. They then had both met with the client's lawyer and handed over the evidence. Agatha worked late, typing up notes on other outstanding cases, and, as she was heading home, that was when Mrs. Bloxby had called her.

"Why do you call Mrs. Bloxby by her surname?" asked Alice, when the interview was over.

"There was a society for women in this village when I arrived here," explained Agatha. "We all addressed each other by surnames and somehow it stuck. I know it's strange these days when every odd and sod calls you by your first name. But I rather like being Mrs. Raisin. I hate when in hospital nurses call me Agatha. Seems overfamiliar, somehow. And, yes, it's ageing, as if they think I'm in my second childhood." She stifled a yawn.

"We'll let you get some sleep," said Bill.

When they had left, Agatha noticed that a red dawn was flooding the kitchen with light. She opened the garden door and let her cats out. The morning was fresh and beautiful. She went into the kitchen and got a wad of paper towel and wiped the dew off a garden lounger and then sank into it, sleepily enjoying the feel of the rising sun on her face and the smell of spring flowers.

She closed her eyes and drifted off to sleep. Two hours later she was in the grip of a nightmare where she had fallen overboard a ship, and as she struggled in the icy water, above her, Jill Davent leaned over the rail and laughed.

She awoke with a start to find the rain was drumming down and she was soaked to the skin. Agatha fled indoors and upstairs, where she stripped off her wet clothes, had a hot shower, pulled on a nightdress and climbed into bed.

Agatha awoke again in the early afternoon and reconnected her phone, which she had switched off before falling asleep. She checked her messages. There were worried ones from her staff and several from the press.

She dressed and went wearily downstairs. Looking through a small opening in the drawn curtains in her front room, she saw the press massed outside her cottage. Agatha went upstairs and changed into an old T-shirt, jacket, loose trousers and running shoes.

Down again and out into the back garden, where she seized a ladder and propped it against the fence. She had somehow planned to heave the ladder up when she was straddled on the top of the fence but could not manage it. She was just about to give up and retreat when James appeared below in the narrow path which separated her cottage from his.

"I'll get my ladder," he called up to her.

If this were a film, thought Agatha grumpily, I would leap down into his strong arms. A watery sunlight was gilding the new leaves of the large lilac tree at the front of her cottage, which mercifully screened her off from the press, which might otherwise have spotted her at the end of the passage.

James came through a side gate from his garden carrying a ladder which he propped against the fence.

Agatha climbed down. She smiled up at James and then ducked her head as she realised she wasn't wearing make-up.

"Come in and have a coffee," said James. "But I really think you should have a word with the press, even if it's 'no comment' or they'll be here all day."

"In these clothes!"

"Agatha! Oh, all right. We'll climb back over, sort yourself out, and then go out to face them."

James waited impatiently in Agatha's kitchen for half an hour until she descended the stairs, fully made-up and teetering on a pair of high heels.

Agatha went out to face the press. She competently fielded questions while television cameras whirred and flashes went off in her face. Yes, she had spent a long time at police headquarters. Why? Because she was a private detective who lived in the village where the woman was murdered.

And then to her horror, Victoria Bannister pushed

her way to the front. "You threatened to kill her!" she shrieked.

"Jill Davent hired a private detective to find out all about me," said Agatha. "I was annoyed with her. That is all. The question that arises is, why was she afraid of me? What had she got to hide?"

"You're a murderer," shouted Victoria.

"And you," said Agatha, "will be hearing from my lawyers. I am going to sue you for slander."

Victoria's wrinkled face showed shock and alarm. "I'm sorry," she babbled. "I made a mistake." She turned to escape, shouting at the press to let her through.

Agatha's voice followed her, "There's one in every village."

And in that moment, Victoria could have killed Agatha. As she fled up to her cottage, she vowed to find out the identity of the murderer herself. She knew all the gossip of the village. Once inside, she poured herself a stiff sherry and went off into a rosy dream where *she* was facing an admiring press and telling them how she had solved the case.

"All done?" asked James as Agatha teetered back into the kitchen, sat down and kicked off her shoes.

"I think they've gone off to the vicarage to persecute Mrs. Bloxby."

"Will she be able to handle it?"

"Oh, yes. A vicar's wife has to be tough. In the past, she's had to confront several women who developed a crush on her husband. It's a lousy existence and she's welcome to it. Half her time is acting as an unpaid therapist. A lot of people take their troubles to her."

"Including you?"

"I'm her friend. That's different. I'll phone Toni to take over tomorrow. I think I'll go into Oxford and talk to Clive."

Clive Tremund's office was in a narrow lane off Walton Street in the Jericho area of Oxford. It was situated in the ground floor of a thin two-storied building. Agatha tried the handle and found the door was unlocked.

There was a little square vestibule with a frosted glass door on the left bearing the legend TREMUND INVESTIGATIONS. She pushed open the door and went in.

Agatha let out a gasp. It was a scene of chaos. Papers were scattered everywhere. Drawers hung open at crazy angles. A filing cabinet had been knocked over onto the floor. She backed slowly out, took out her phone and called the police. Then she went outside to wait.

The cobbled lane was very quiet.

After only five minutes, a police car rolled to a stop

and two policemen got out. Agatha quickly told them who she was, why she had called and what she had found. The police called it in. Another wait while two detectives arrived. Agatha had to make her statement again and was told to wait until a forensic team arrived.

The day was becoming darker and a damp gusty wind promised rain. Agatha retreated to her car and lit a cigarette, noticing that her fingers were shaking. Where was Clive? What had happened to him? She felt in need of support. Agatha noticed that neighbours were emerging from the surrounding houses. She phoned Toni and asked her to join her, saying, "Pretend to be a curious onlooker and question the neighbours before you come and talk to me."

A forensic team arrived and suited up before going into the office. The morning dragged on. At last Toni arrived and Agatha could see her questioning the neighbours. Then Toni finally walked off and disappeared around the corner into Walton Street while Agatha fretted. Where on earth was she going?

After ten minutes, Toni returned, carrying a large brown paper bag. She slid into the passenger seat of Agatha's car.

"Coffee and sticky buns," said Toni, opening the bag.

"You're an angel. What did you get from the neighbours?"

"Not much. He lived upstairs."

"Oh, snakes and bastards!" howled Agatha. "I didn't even think to have a look. He could be lying dead up there."

"Don't think so. No ambulance. Have a bun."

"Ta. So what else?"

"Didn't speak to the neighbours. His clients mostly called in the evenings. Yesterday evening, one young woman, blond, slim, that's all the description."

"Could be you," said Agatha gloomily.

"Two men at different intervals, both looking like middle-aged businessmen, one tall and thin and the other small and tubby. Not much to go on."

"I should have looked for a client list," mourned Agatha, "instead of rushing out to phone the police. But you know how it is, one fingerprint and they'd haul me in for breaking and entering. I'll come back when things have quietened down and try the next-door neighbours. The police are already knocking at doors."

"That's why I couldn't try them myself," said Toni. "All I could do was to pretend to be one of the crowd. Have another bun. They're very comforting."

"Oh, well, why not?"

There came a rapping on Agatha's window. The detective who had interviewed her earlier said, "You are to come with me to Thames Valley Police to be interviewed. Leave your car here. An officer will drive you back. Who is this young lady?"

Oh, to be young and beautiful, thought Agatha grumpily. The man's practically leering.

"Miss Toni Gilmour," said Agatha. "One of my detectives."

"She'd better come with you. I don't want anyone messing up this crime scene."

Agatha made her statement again to a refreshingly young and efficient female detective. She was just about to leave when the ax fell. She was told that she had to recover her car and then drive to Mircester police headquarters and make another statement, and Agatha knew that Wilkes's idea of an interview could run into hours.

There was no sign of Toni. Agatha got into her car and phoned her.

"I got chased away," said Toni. "I'll come back this evening, if you like."

"Let me think about that. Do you know if they've found Clive?"

"Not a sign of him. A friendly policeman told me his flat was empty before he got reprimanded."

"I hope to God he's all right," said Agatha. "I've got to go to Mircester to make another statement. I'll call you tomorrow."

Agatha knew the rush-hour traffic would be building

up and so she decided to drive to the Botley road and exit Oxford by the ring road.

But as she got to the bottom of Beaufort Street, the traffic slowed to a stop and she could see police erecting a barrier.

She swung off into the Gloucester Green car park and then made her way on foot to the barrier. "I must get past," she said to a policeman on duty. "My train's about to leave," she lied, quickly thinking of an excuse to find out what had happened.

"All right. But keep clear of the police activity on the canal bridge. There are enough rubberneckers there already."

Agatha hurried down Worcester Street to Hythe Bridge Street. "What's up?" Agatha asked a man.

"Body in the canal," he said.

With a feeling of dread, Agatha elbowed her way to the front, ignoring angry protests. A weak sun was gilding the black waters of the canal. As Agatha watched, the sun shone down on the dead face of Clive Tremund as his body was dragged from the water.

She realised that if she was spotted by any detectives who had been at Clive's house, then there would be more questions, and so she shoved her way back through the crowd.

Agatha felt miserable as she drove to Mircester. Clive had been her one hope of getting a break in the case. Once she got to Mircester and before she went into police headquarters, she phoned Patrick Mulligan and briefed him on what had been happening. "See if your old police contacts can tell you anything," said Agatha.

As the long interview progressed, Agatha realised to her horror that Wilkes was beginning to regard her as the number-one suspect. He seemed to believe that Agatha had searched Tremund's offices herself, because there was something in her past she did not want anyone to know.

After fifteen minutes, Agatha lost her temper. "I want a lawyer," she shouted.

She was escorted to a waiting room where she phoned criminal lawyer Sir David Herythe. She had met David at a party on one of her brief visits to London the year before. Agatha had found him very attractive, so, she thought, why not kill two birds with one stone. She knew he commuted to London from Oxford.

He listened patiently to her furious tirade and then to her relief, he said he was actually in Oxford and would be right over. David knew that Agatha had a knack of getting into situations which drew in a lot of publicity and David loved to see his own photograph in the newspapers.

He arrived half an hour later and walked with

Agatha to the interview room. He was a tall man with silver hair and a high-bridged nose. He was famous for his waspish remarks in court.

He quickly established that Agatha had not been charged with anything, that she had already made a full statement to the Oxford police, suggested they read the report and stop wasting his client's time, smiled all round and ushered Agatha out.

"Let's have dinner," he said. "The George?" And without waiting for a reply, he set off with long rangy strides. Agatha raced to keep up with him.

As the evening was fine and warm, the earlier miserable weather having cleared, they found a table on the terrace overlooking the hotel gardens.

Agatha lit a cigarette and studied her companion's face. He was examining the menu as if reading a brief. His face was lightly tanned.

"Been on holiday?" asked Agatha.

"Yes, Monaco, at a friend's place. Be with you in a minute. Food is a serious business. I'm going to be very conventional. I'll have the lobster salad followed by tournedos Rossini. Oh, how grand. They have a bottle of Chateau Montelena Sauvignon 2010."

Agatha blinked rapidly, recognising the wine as the most expensive on the menu.

Not another cheapskate, she thought. He's going to stiff me with the bill. She realised she was very tired and that her make-up needed repair. But what did it all matter, she grumbled to herself, with dead bodies following me around like wasps?

"I'll have the same," she said.

He waved an imperious hand to summon the waiter and gave the order.

Agatha could only be thankful that he had not ordered another bottle of wine to accompany the first course.

"Now," he said, "tell me all about it."

Agatha gave him a succinct report without her usual exaggerations.

When she had finished, he said, "So we have a therapist with dicey credentials, who, nonetheless, must have had a strong personality to draw in quite a few clients. Can you think of anyone in the village amongst the people who consulted her who might be a murderer?"

"It can't be my cleaner, Mrs. Simpson. Too decent and honourable. I would like it to be Victoria Bannister because she's a malicious old cow. Mrs. Tweedy, I don't know, but she is elderly. But my money's on Gwen Simple. Remember her? Son put people in meat pies?"

The first course arrived and they both concentrated on eating it, Agatha finding that she was very hungry.

Then he surprised her by saying, "I could be of help to you. I have seen so many criminals. I have not yet finished my holiday. If you like, I could visit the four clients that you know of and see what conclusions I come to."

Agatha hesitated. "I would not charge you a fee," he said. "It would be a sort of busman's holiday."

Looking at him with new eyes, Agatha realised he was an attractive man. Was he married?

When the main course arrived, he turned all his attention to the food and wine, leaving Agatha to eat her dinner automatically and dream of being married to him. And wouldn't that put Charles's nose out of joint!

By the end of the meal, he had taken a note of the names and addresses of the three women who had consulted Jill. He had a good contact in the police in Oxford and felt sure he could find out a lot about Clive Tremund.

More than that, he paid the bill!

He escorted Agatha back to her car in the square and said he would call on her in her office on the following afternoon.

When she arrived home, Agatha patted her cats, fed them, and then rushed to her computer to look up Sir David Herythe. He had been married to a glamorous model but the marriage had ended in an amicable divorce.

Rats, thought Agatha, dismally looking at a photograph of the ex-wife. She was blond and beautiful. If his taste ran to arm candy, there wasn't much hope for one middle-aged detective.

Mind you, there weren't any children and that—

"How's it going?" asked Charles from behind her. Agatha leapt up in alarm. "What are you doing here?" she demanded.

"Heard about Tremund's murder and came to hold your hand. Why are you looking up Sir David Herythe?"

"I employed him," said Agatha, "to get me out of the clutches of Wilkes, who seems to think I go around murdering people."

"He's wickedly expensive," said Charles.

Agatha switched off her computer and moved to the drinks table.

"If you're having a nightcap," said Charles, "get me a brandy."

Agatha poured two goblets of brandy and handed one to Charles. She sat down beside him on the sofa.

"Listen to this, my miserly friend," she said. "He not only paid for a very expensive dinner at the George, but he has a week's holiday left and is going to detect for me. For nothing!"

"Oh, do be careful, Aggie. He tears people apart."

"That's his job. He prosecutes people."

"I'm not talking about his behaviour in court. I've met him before at several parties. He befriends someone, usually a woman, and when his interest dies, he mocks her in public."

Agatha felt a qualm of unease. Then she rallied. "Look, I need all the help I can get."

The next morning, Agatha, who had gone up to bed telling Charles to lock up on his way out, was irritated to find him sitting at the breakfast table. What if David should drop by?

"I thought you had left," she said grumpily.

"I'm bored," said Charles, lifting Hodge off his knee. "I thought I'd join you in a bit of detecting."

Agatha hesitated. Then she remembered the magic of Charles's title had been the means before of gaining good interviews. "But buy your own cigarettes," she added as she tried to move her packet of Bensons out of his reach. She wasn't quick enough and he extracted one and lit it.

Producing an electronic cigarette from her handbag, Agatha fiercely inhaled.

"Oh, have a real one," urged Charles. "You may not

40

get cancer but you'll give yourself a hernia trying to get a hit from one of those."

"I must give up," fretted Agatha. "It's so yesterday to smoke. Not to mention the smell."

Charles blew a smoke ring and smiled lazily at her. He rose to his feet and let the cats out into the garden. "No need for the pets to suffer."

"I thought of trying Mrs. Tweedy first. She's reported to be very old but she may be able to tell us something about Jill. I'll have a coffee and then we'll take a walk up there."

Mrs. Tweedy lived in a cul-de-sac at the back of the vicarage in a row of Georgian cottages. There was no bell. Agatha seized a brass knocker in the shape of a lion's head and hammered with it.

The door opened and an elderly woman surveyed her. Agatha introduced herself and Charles and they were invited in. Mrs. Tweedy led them through a small dining area to her living room. The room was very dark because of the ivy which covered the windows. Flickering sunlight, shining through the ivy leaves, danced about the room, which was sparsely furnished with a three-piece suite covered in chintz and a small television set. Mrs. Tweedy was a thickset woman with grey hair and a pugnacious face. She was wearing a dress with a chintz pattern, like the furniture. Her long, gnarled fingers were covered in diamond rings. Her thick black-stockinged legs ended in a pair of tartan slippers. Her eyes were small and shrewd.

"We want to ask you for your impression of Jill Davent," Agatha began.

"People are saying you killed her," said Mrs. Tweedy.

"Well, I didn't," said Agatha. "What did you make of her?"

"Good listener. No one listens to the old these days. In fact, nobody listens to anyone these days. While you're talking to them, all they do is wait for you to finish so they can talk about themselves."

"Is that the only reason you went to her?" asked Charles. "To get someone to listen to you?"

"And what's up with that, may I ask?"

"Not a thing," said Charles. "What did you make of her?"

"Silly bitch!" said Mrs. Tweedy venomously.

"What? Why do you say that?" asked Agatha.

"Last session, I was talking about my life. I miss my brother, who died in an accident. I was living in Oxford and decided to move to the country because cities can be lonely places. Well, I was talking and her phone rang. She took it out into the hall and shut the door. I went to the door and listened. She must have been talking to a fellow because it was 'darling this' and 'darling that.' Then she came back in and said the session was over and tried to charge me. I told her to get stuffed. Never went back. I wish I had never come here. This village is creepy and you, Agatha Raisin, are one of the creepiest things about it—entertaining your fancy man here at nights." She glared at Charles.

"You ought to make an honest woman of her."

Before Agatha could say anything, Charles smiled and said, "You are one truly horrible woman."

Mrs. Tweedy let out a cackle of laughter. "I like a man who speaks his mind."

"And I hate old frumps who speak theirs!" yelled Agatha. "I'm getting out of this dump!"

As they left, they were followed by roars of laughter from the old lady.

"Ah, the dignity and grace of old age," said Charles as they walked through the village. "Let's visit Mrs. Bloxby and see if she's picked up some gossip. Also, you should let Bill know about that 'darling' phone call. Pity we haven't the means to trace it. I mean, if she carried the phone out it must have been on her mobile and that'll be in the evidence locker."

"Not necessarily," said Agatha. "It could be one of those hands-free phones and it might still be there. If only we could break in and have a look. You can find out recent phone calls. I wonder who inherits? Wait a moment and I'll phone Patrick and see if he's found out anything."

Charles wandered up to the road. People were coming and going from the village shop. It all looked like a rural idyll. In the old days, he thought, Agatha would be blamed for attracting murder and burnt at the stake.

"That's interesting," said Agatha, coming to join him. "Her brother inherits. He's called Adrian Sommerville and he lives in Mircester. He's an interior decorator and I've got the address."

"Oh, well, bang goes tea and sympathy at the vicarage," said Charles. "We'll take your car."

"Meaning, you'll take my petrol, cheapskate."

"You're slipping, Aggie," commented Charles as they approached Mircester. "You should have looked up Sommerville in the phone book."

"Don't tell me how to do my job," said Agatha huffily. "I've got the address. I don't need to phone. Let's see. He's got a business address in The Loans. That's the lane by the abbey. We'll park in the main square and walk."

There was a brass plaque outside the door with the legend SOMERVILLE INTERIORS. A small sign said, PRESS BELL AND ENTER.

Inside, a blonde was sitting behind a reception desk. She put down a copy of *House* & *Garden*, smiled at them and asked how she could be of assistance.

Agatha performed the introductions, wishing not for the first time that she was in the police force and could just flash a warrant card.

The secretary disappeared into an interior office. They waited.

Agatha was just saying, "Do you think he's escaped out the back?" when the blonde returned.

"Mr. Sommerville can spare you a few moments," she said grandly, radiating disapproval from every thread of her tailored power suit.

Adrian Sommerville came as a surprise. Agatha was expecting some sort of willowy stereotype, but the man who rose to shake hands with them was dark and squat, wearing a sober grey suit, silk shirt and tie. He had a thick thatch of black hair, thick lips and designer stubble. He was seated behind an antique desk. Agatha and Charles sat down on chairs facing him. The walls of the office were decorated with photos of expensive-looking rooms.

His first question surprised Agatha. "Who is paying you?"

"No one," said Agatha. "The murder took place in my village and I want to know who did it."

"I hear the police suspect you."

"Well, I didn't murder anyone," retorted Agatha crossly. "I wouldn't be wasting my time otherwise."

"Unless to throw them off the scent."

Agatha half rose to her feet but Charles pulled her down.

"Stop being so aggressive," he said. "Don't you want to find out who murdered your Jill?"

"Of course I do. But it's better to leave it to the police."

"We're sorry for your loss," said Charles. "But it's a loss you don't seem to be grieving over. What do you plan to do with her house?"

"Sell it. Why?"

"I might like to buy it," said Charles. "I collect properties. Hobby of mine. How much?"

"Five hundred thousand or so."

"Rubbish," said Charles. "A nasty little cottage where a murder has taken place? Three hundred thousand?"

"It's not on the market yet." Adrian's eyes held a mercenary gleam.

"I might like to have a look at it," said Charles.

"You own that big place in Warwickshire, don't you?"

"Yes."

"Give me your card. I'll phone you when the police have finished with it. Don't want to bother with blood-sucking estate agents, now do we?"

"Of course not."

"So, goodbye."

Charles could feel the volcano that was Agatha simmering beside him.

He handed Adrian his card and heaved Agatha out of her chair. "Let's go, darling."

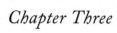

Chapter Three

Outside, Agatha raged, "Horrible man!"

"Oh, calm down," said Charles. "We want a look inside her cottage, don't we? You nearly spoiled things."

"I am sorry," said Agatha in a suddenly mild voice. Charles looked at her suspiciously. Agatha had just remembered that David Herythe was due to call at her office and she didn't want Charles around. "Why don't we split up? I can't interview Victoria because she'll just curse me. But you could and we could meet up later."

"All right," said Charles reluctantly. "What are you going to do?"

"I've got to get to the office and see how the others are getting on. I do have a business to run, Charles, and no one is paying me for all this effort."

"But we came in your car, or have you forgotten? How am I to get to Carsely?"

Agatha whipped out her mobile phone. "Toni," she said, "could you be an angel and run Charles back to Carsely? Great. We'll meet you in the car park."

Now, why doesn't Agatha want me in her office? wondered Charles. "We haven't had anything to eat," he said. "Why don't we all go for a late lunch?" he asked as Toni came hurrying towards them.

"I'm not hungry," lied Agatha. "Why don't you and Toni go for a bite first?"

"I've already had lunch," said Toni.

"You can watch me eat," said Charles.

They were about to walk off, when Toni called, "My wits are wandering. Herythe is waiting for you in the office, Agatha."

Charles gave a malicious smile. "I haven't seen David in ages. Must say hullo," and to Agatha's horror, he set off for her office without waiting for her.

Toni and Agatha hurried after him.

To Agatha's further irritation, when she got to the office it was to find David Herythe seated behind her desk and going through the contents of her computer.

"Charles Fraith!" cried David. "What are you doing here?"

While Charles explained that he was a close friend of Agatha's and the conversation turned to the sort of do-you-know about people Agatha had never met, she leaned over and switched off her computer. Still talking, David vacated her desk and walked round to join Charles.

"Why don't we go for a drink?" said Charles.

"Great idea." Both men headed for the door.

"Stop!" shouted Agatha.

They both turned around. Charles smiled at her sweetly and David raised his eyebrows.

"I mean," said Agatha desperately, "you were supposed to find out something for me, David."

"Oh, that. I've got as far as finding out how Tremund was murdered. He wasn't strangled. He was struck on the head with some blunt instrument. A bag of stones was slung round his neck and he was tipped into the canal. The divers found it when they brought him up."

"How did they know he was in the canal?" asked Agatha. "And when was he shoved in?"

"They haven't done the pathology thoroughly yet, but some students have finally come forward. They said it was about three in the morning and they were coming back from a party when they heard a splash from the canal. One girl said she thought she saw a man's head above the water and then it disappeared."

"Why didn't they come forward sooner?" asked Agatha.

"The police guess they had been on drugs and didn't want to get involved, but one of them, a girl called Hayley Martin, got a fit of conscience and called in at the police station and reported what they had seen."

"Did she see anyone else around?" asked Toni.

"She saw a dark figure on the towpath but couldn't see if it was a man or a woman. Her friends told her to forget it, that it was just someone fly tipping.

"I went to see this Hayley Martin. I told her that anything she told me would not be reported to the police. She said the others were drunk and had been smoking pot. She said she didn't take drugs and hadn't had all that much to drink. I could see why the police took her story seriously. She's a very pretty girl and very honest.

"Now, to Tremund's office. His computer has been taken and as you saw, Agatha, papers and correspondence were scattered all over the place."

"Did the police say whether Jill Davent kept tapes of her sessions?"

"Evidently she didn't. That's all I've got. Come along,

Charles. All this talking has given me a thirst. I'll be in touch, Agatha."

Over drinks in the George, David said, "Are you in a relationship with that Raisin woman?"

"We are very close friends."

"Didn't think it could be anything else," said David. "Why?"

"Men like us can have a pick of the young ones," said David. "Though I must admit Agatha is sexy. Might have a fling there."

Charles rose to his feet. His light voice carried around the bar.

"Don't you dare!"

"Why?"

"Because I'll kill you," said Charles and strode out of the hotel bar.

David Herythe was furious. People treated him with respect. He would bed Agatha and make sure Fraith heard about it.

He finished his drink and decided to return to his home in Summertown in Oxford.

He lived in a Victorian villa, one of the ones that had been built for the Oxford dons in the nineteenth century when the decision was made to allow them to live out of college and marry. It is the most expensive part of

Oxford. He also had an apartment in the Inner Temple in London, one of the Inns of Court.

He parked his car in the short drive under a laburnum tree and got out, savouring the peace of the evening. He let himself in, reset the burglar alarm, went to the kitchen and poured himself a glass of Chardonnay and carried it through to his desk in the office.

He started to make out a bill for his services at police headquarters to send to Agatha. That being done he opened the window wide, for the evening was warm, listening to the blackbirds singing and the hiss of traffic going down the Banbury road.

His phone rang. A gruff, sexless voice said, "If you want to know who done those murders, meet me at the Hythe Bridge canal in half an hour." Then whoever it was rang off.

Now this is either some nutter or the real murderer, thought David. He phoned the police and told them about the call. They said they would send plainclothes detectives to keep watch.

As he got into his car and set off, he felt the thrill of the chase. He parked in the Worcester Road car park and walked round to Hythe Bridge. He could not recognise the detectives, but the road was busy with young people coming and going. As the time dragged past, he realised the call must have been a hoax. He phoned the police and said he had been the victim of a silly trick and he was going home.

As he parked, he noticed to his irritation that he had left his office window open in his excitement. He let himself in, reset the burglar alarm and decided to make himself an omelette before going to bed.

After he had eaten, he undressed, showered and went to bed. But he felt restless, tossing and turning until he decided to take two of his prescribed sleeping pills, the ones he had been trying so hard to do without.

With a sigh of relief, he settled back against the pillows. Soon his eyes closed and he was fast asleep.

He slept naked. A gloved hand came out of the darkness and gently pulled the covers down. Leaves were pressed against his chest. The figure moved silently away.

David jerked awake as palpitations racked his body. His body arched in convulsions, he writhed in agony and then fell into a coma.

The dark figure came back and picked the leaves from his body and then disappeared.

David Herythe's cleaning woman, Mrs. Danby, let herself in the following morning. She reset the burglar alarm and went into the kitchen, hoping to be able to have a cup of tea before Mr. Herythe, whom she knew to be an early riser, descended the stairs.

She was not only able to have a cup of tea in peace but a cigarette as well. Then she began to clean the downstairs. When, by midmorning, her employer did not appear, she began to become worried. His car was in the drive. Heaving the old vacuum up the stairs and cursing her employer for being too mean to buy one of the newer, lighter ones, she left the machine on the landing and pushed open David's bedroom door.

A shaft of sunlight shining in between a gap in the heavy curtains shone full on the twisted rictus of agony that was David's face.

Mrs. Danby backed slowly away. She knew she should check for a pulse but she was too frightened to go anywhere near that awful death mask. She retreated to the landing and slammed the door, scrabbled in the pocket of her old trousers for her phone and called the police before going downstairs on shaky legs to cut off the burglar alarm and leave the door open.

Two police cars arrived, then three detectives and then the pathologist, followed closely by a forensic team, whose job it was to go over the whole house, while Mrs. Danby sat on a kitchen chair in the front garden, shivering despite the warmth of the day.

Agatha allowed a small television in the corner of her office to play the BBC's twenty-four-hour news service, so long as the volume was turned low. She was just saying to Phil, "Get your cameras and we'll try that adultery case again," when Phil said, "Listen!" He went over and turned up the sound on the television. David Herythe's face came up on the screen, dressed in wig and gown. "His body was found at his home in Oxford by his cleaner, Mrs. Danby," the announcer was saying, "but the police do not suspect foul play. Preliminary reports suggest that the eminent barrister died of a massive heart attack."

"Don't believe it," said Agatha. "Where's Patrick?"

"At the supermarket, checking out the staff to see who's been nicking the electric goods."

Agatha phoned him and told him about Herythe. "Have you any contacts in the Thames Valley Police?" she asked.

"I've got one. I'll see what I can find out."

Agatha rang off and turned to Simon. "Find out this Mrs. Danby's address and get over there. It must be murder."

It was evening before Simon was able to track down the cleaner who lived in tower block on the Blackbird Leys council estate. The door was opened by a young woman with an improbable colour of aubergine hair, two nose rings, and holding a screaming baby.

"Mrs. Danby?" asked Simon.

"Naw, she ain't speaking to no press, so get lost."

"I'm not press. I'm a detective," said Simon.

"Oh, well, that's different. Hey, Beryl," she called, "another of them police."

Simon knew he should reveal his proper identity but he decided to do that as he was leaving.

He was ushered into a filthy living room, showing that some cleaners can't be bothered with their own homes after they've finished cleaning someone else's. Empty pizza boxes littered the floor, empty beer cans spilled over out of a plastic bin in the corner and old newspapers and magazines were piled up everywhere.

The woman with the baby said, "I'm off home, Mum, to get Frank's tea. I'll be round in the morning."

When she had gone, Simon said, "Just a few questions, Mrs. Danby."

"Could you give me a minute to change?" said Mrs. Danby. She raised one powerful freckled arm and sniffed her armpit. "I stink something awful."

"Go ahead," said Simon. When she had gone, he opened a window wide because it wasn't only Mrs. Danby's armpits that stank.

Mrs. Danby went into her bedroom and stripped off her blouse and trousers. Her trousers were too long for her and she had rolled up the bottoms. She took the trousers and threw them on top of a pile of clothes in the laundry basket. A large leaf which had been stuck to the bottom of the trousers fell at her feet. She automatically picked it up and rolled it between her fingers while she wondered if she had anything clean to wear.

She suddenly clutched her heart as she was seized by a violent allergic reaction. "Help!" she shrieked.

Simon came running in, looked at her contorted face and wondered why the matronly Mrs. Danby was wearing a scarlet thong. He phoned for an ambulance.

Desperate to do something, he went into the kitchen, filled a glass of water, poured a pile of salt into it, mixed it up and took it to her. "Drink!" he shouted. He got her to take a large gulp and then she vomited all over the floor. "Did you eat or drink something bad?" he asked.

"Leaf," she said weakly. "That there leaf."

Simon heard the wail of a siren. He took out a little plastic back and put on gloves. He lifted the leaf carefully into the bag.

"What's your daughter's phone number?" he asked.

"On the wall. Above the kitchen phone. Josie Maller."

The ambulance men arrived, closely followed by two policemen and a detective. The woman was Detective Sergeant Ruby Carson. She had blond hair and deep blue eyes. Simon forgot all about Toni and fell in love on the spot. He rapidly told Ruby and the paramedics about the leaf. She said she would take his statement while waiting for the pathologist and a forensic team to arrive, while they sat in her car.

Said Ruby, after Simon had reverently handed her the little plastic bag with the leaf inside, "I'll phone the hospital in a few minutes to make sure she's still alive. I'll give this leaf to the forensic lab." She took his statement down, printed it off on her mobile printer and got him to sign it.

"It all seems to have started in that village where your boss lives," said Ruby. "What's the connection?"

"David Herythe was on holiday and keen to do a bit of detecting," said Simon. "He dies. His cleaning woman picks up this discarded leaf and has a seizure. Jill Davent, that therapist, I am sure, found out something about someone, and whatever it was panicked a murderer."

"I'll just phone the hospital." Simon waited while

Ruby phoned, studying her attractive profile. How old was she? Maybe a good bit older than he was. He wondered whether to ask her out.

She finally rang off and said that Mrs. Danby was still alive.

Simon took the plunge. "What do you do in your spare time?" he asked.

Ruby flashed him an amused look. "Are you chatting me up?"

"Trying to," said Simon.

There was a rap at the car window. "Detective Inspector Briggs, Mr. Black," said a man, leaning in the passenger window. "Have you made a statement?"

"Yes."

"Well, you are to go directly to Mircester police headquarters and tell them what you've been up to." Off with you."

When he had left, Simon groaned. "They'll probably keep me up all night. Do you have a card?"

Ruby smiled and handed one over.

"Thanks," said Simon. "I'll be in touch."

She isn't wearing any rings, he thought happily, as he drove off to Mircester.

Unaware of what was going on, Agatha sat in her own cleaner's cosy parlour and asked, "Why did you consult

Jill Davent? I would have thought you were the last person to need a therapist."

"I met her in the village shop," said Doris Simpson. Her cat, Scrabble, jumped on her capacious lap and settled down to sleep. "I had been suffering with pains in my shoulders. She said it was tension and she could take the pain away. Well, the doctor couldn't find nothing wrong so I thought I'd give it a try. She massaged my shoulders and said she was taking all my tension away. Then she not only made me cough up sixty pounds but charged me twenty for the massage oil."

"If you are suffering from tension, you're worried. Out with it."

"I'm right ashamed. We decided to buy this council house, but I was overambitious, like. I'm behind with the payments and the bank is threatening to repossess."

Agatha thought rapidly. The council houses were good solid property.

"Who would you have left it to, if you had succeeded in buying it?"

"We haven't even made a will, Agatha. We couldn't have children and there's no one close."

"Well, here's what we'll do," said Agatha. "I'll buy it, but you live in it till the end of your days. I'll put a codicil in my will to that effect. We'll see the lawyers and bank tomorrow."

"But your job is dangerous! What if me and hubby outlive you? You won't get any benefit."

Agatha hadn't thought of that. On the other hand, Doris was a superb cleaner and she looked after Agatha's cats when Agatha was away.

She shrugged. "Oh, let's go for it. Deal?"

"Oh, Agatha! You're a saint. May you live forever."

But out in the nighttime darkness of the Cotswolds, someone was already planning to send Agatha Raisin to an early grave.

Chapter Four

Everything seemed to grind to a halt. Spring moved into summer. Agatha could not find out the results of Mrs. Danby's illness, except that somehow it was because she had picked up a leaf. But what type of leaf? Agatha could not understand why it was taking them so long to identify it.

The fact was, as Patrick Mulligan was at last able to find out, that the leaf had somehow become lost in the forensic lab. How?

A young forensic scientist who had gone on holiday was eventually tracked down to one of the Greek islands. At first she claimed to know nothing about it, but under the grilling of two Thames Valley detectives, who were determined not to find out that their journey had been unnecessary, burst into tears and confessed she had opened the lab window to call down to her boyfriend and several bits and pieces had blown out.

A hurried and frantic search of all the debris below that window at last revealed the little envelope blown up against a wire fence.

This Simon was also able to tell Agatha because he was in constant touch with Ruby, although, so far, he had not persuaded her to come out on a date with him.

The leaf was at last identified as coming from monkshood, a deadly killer of a plant. It was once used to kill wolves and mad dogs and was then called wolfsbane. All parts of the plant are poisonous and it doesn't even need to be taken by mouth; the poison can be absorbed through the skin. It looks like a delphinium and the most common colour is purple.

"So are they going to exhume Herythe's body?" asked Agatha one morning as he staff were gathered in the office.

"No point," said Patrick. "It's the perfect killer and the poison doesn't stay in the body. But the police are regarding it as murder and Charles has been pulled in for questioning."

"Why Charles, of all people?"

"Someone tipped off the police that he was heard threatening to kill Herythe in the bar of the George."

"I'd better get round there and see if there's anything I can do," said Agatha.

She was about to leave when there came a tentative knock on the door. Agatha opened it and found herself faced with a small boy carrying a bouquet of flowers. "Are you Mrs. Raisin?" he asked.

"That's me."

"These are for you."

Agatha was just reaching for the bouquet when Toni shrieked, "Don't touch it. You, boy, drop it on the floor."

Startled, the boy did as he was told.

"Look at the flowers," said Toni. "That looks like monkshood."

"Who gave you those flowers?" asked Agatha.

The boy was small and fair-haired. "It was a big chap. He gave me ten pounds to deliver them."

The flowers were wrapped in gold paper. "Did you touch the flowers anywhere?" Patrick asked the boy.

"N-no."

"The stems are wrapped up so he should be all right," said Patrick. "I'll call the police."

"What's your name?" Agatha asked the boy.

"Jimmy Martin, miss."

"Look, Jimmy, go into the toilet over there and wash your hands thoroughly. That bouquet may be poisonous.

You'll need to wait here. The police will want to interview you."

"Like in the fillums?"

"Just like that."

"Wicked!"

There was a long delay, waiting for the boy's mother to
arrive before he could be interviewed. His description
of the big man who had given him the flowers was
vague. But it had taken place at the corner of market
square, which was covered by a video camera. Not for
the first time, Agatha fretted at not having the powers
of the police. She would dearly have loved to have a look
at the videotape.

When it was all over, and the boy had been taken
home by his mother, Charles strolled in.

Agatha told him about the latest development.
The usually urbane and unflappable Charles looked
worried. "So you're the killer's new target. You'd better
take a holiday, Agatha."

"Not me," said Agatha. "Patrick, take money out of
the petty cash and stand drinks for your old police buddies and find out what's on that video."

"Too soon," said Patrick. "Give it a few hours. I'll get
on with that divorce case and then I'll let you know if
I find out anything."

"So, Charles," said Agatha, "how did you get on?"

"Wilkes was really nasty," said Charles. "The press are breathing down his neck. He all but accused me outright. Come on, Aggie. I could do with a drink."

"Too early."

"The sun is over the poop deck or whatever."

"Wait until I arrange things here. What have we got, Toni?"

"Simon and I have that missing girl. Patrick's got his divorce case and Phil is going with him to take pictures. And you forgot about yourself. So you have some free time."

"All right, Charles," said Agatha. "One drink and then I'll get back here and go through my notes."

In the pub, Agatha surveyed Charles over the rim of her glass. There he sat, impeccably tailored and barbered, as if they had never known a few nights of passion. Agatha's hands began to shake and she carefully put her glass down on the table. "Take a deep breath," said Charles. "It's not every day someone tries to kill you, although it sometimes begins to look like that. Be sensible. Go away for a long holiday. Leave it to the police for once."

"It would haunt me," said Agatha. She carefully lifted her glass again and took a swig of gin and tonic.

"There must be something in Jill Davent's past. I find my mind has been blocked by Gwen Simple. I want her to be guilty. I feel she got away with murder. So who else have I got? There are the ones in the village who consulted Jill. Bannister's a vicious old bitch but I can't see her as a murderer. Doris wouldn't harm a fly and Mrs. Tweedy's too old. I took a note of Jill's old address in Mircester. I think I'll go there and ferret around. There must be some reason she moved to Carsely. Why leave a big town where she could have found many more clients? She paused. "Why were the police questioning you?"

"I threatened to kill Herythe and was overheard."

"Why?"

Charles didn't want to tell her that he had lost his temper when Herythe had threatened to seduce her. "Oh, he got on my nerves. I had forgotten how waspish he could be. Take someone with you to Mircester," urged Charles. "I've got to go home. Got a meeting with the land agent."

"I'll be all right," said Agatha. "I think I'll be safe now."

"But for how long?" asked Charles. "What about your cats?"

"What about them?"

"You get your milk delivered, don't you? Little bit of poison injected into the bottle."

"All right. I'll take them to Doris. I swear they like her better than me. I forgot to ask you. How did you get on with the Bannister woman?"

"Nothing but spite and malice. Two sandwiches short of a picnic."

Outside the pub, Charles paused for a moment and watched Agatha as she walked to her car. She was wearing a short linen skirt, which showed her excellent legs to advantage. He had begged Wilkes to give her police protection, but Wilkes had said brutally that he had no intention of wasting manpower on a woman who had chosen a dangerous job. Charles decided to call on her that evening, although he rationed his visits to Agatha. It was, he told himself, no use becoming overfond of a woman who was a walking obsession constantly searching for a host. Agatha's habit of falling in love with highly unsuitable men had irritated him in the past. He wondered gloomily who the next one would be.

What had once been Jill's consulting rooms was now a handbag shop. A man with a thick moustache and an even thicker Eastern European accent approached her and asked if she would like to see any of the bags.

"No," said Agatha. She handed over her card. "I'm interested in the therapist who used to have an office here. Did you buy the premises from her?"

"No, I rent, see. Don't know no therapist."

"Who do you rent from?"

"Harcourt and Gentle."

"Where can I find them?"

"In the shopping arcade."

Mircester's shopping arcade was an uninspiring place, half full of closed shops. The other half boasted chain stores and the estate agent.

Agatha pushed open the door and went in. A tall woman was sitting at a desk. She had grey hair and was wearing old-fashioned harlequin glasses. Agatha thought she looked remarkably like Dame Edna Everidge.

"Take a seat, dear," said the woman. "You can call me Jenny. What can I do you for? That's my little joke. We like to put our customers at ease. Some poor souls are forced to downsize and Jenny's here to hold their poor hands. Why I remember, just the other day—"

"Stop!" commanded Agatha. "I am a private detective and would like some information about one of your previous clients."

"Naughty, naughty! Jenny does not give out information about clients."

"And Agatha would like to point out to Jenny that this client was brutally murdered."

"Oh, Jill Davent! Such a tragedy. I wept buckets. I'm ever so sensitive."

The door opened and a tubby, balding man bustled in. "It's all right, Mother," he said. "Thanks for minding the shop. You can go home now. Ah, here's your nurse."

A muscular woman came in and led Jenny away. "I'm James Harcourt," said the man, sitting down in the chair his mother had vacated. "I don't know how Mother got the key to this place or how she got out of the home. I locked up and went out for only ten minutes."

"Which home is your mother in?" asked Agatha.

"Sunnydale. So what are you looking for?"

Agatha handed over her card and explained the reason for her visit.

"I really can't tell you anything," he said. "She took a short lease for only six months."

"Where was she before that?"

"Some address in Evesham."

"Would you please let me have it?"

"I gave all the documents to the police. You'll need to ask them."

"Snakes and bastards!" muttered Agatha outside the estate agent's. "Fat chance of the police letting me see anything."

A mother walking past pulled her child away. "I've told you. Don't stare at crazy people."

That's it, thought Agatha. I'm sure Jenny Harcourt is only eccentric. Sunnydale. I'll give it a try.

She checked on her iPad. Sunnydale was situated a few miles outside Mircester. Agatha got into her car and drove there. As she stopped in the car park, she wondered how to introduce herself. She doubted very much whether they would let a detective interview a mentally disabled patient.

At the reception desk, she said she was Mrs. Harcourt's cousin. A male nurse behind the desk looked at her doubtfully. "Mrs. Harcourt went wandering off today. She has her good days and bad days. Wait here."

Agatha took a seat and looked sadly around. We all live so long these days, she thought, that unless you're very lucky, you can lose all your marbles. What would I do? Would I even know I was dotty?

The nurse came back. "I think it's all right. Mrs. Harcourt will be pleased to see you."

This is not bad, thought Agatha. Mrs. Harcourt had a sunny room with a view of lawns and trees. There were a few pieces of antique furniture she had been allowed to bring with her.

"How nice to see you again so soon," said Jenny Harcourt. "Jenny was talking about Jill Davent."

"Why are you not allowed to leave the home?" asked Agatha

"I have a little problem, but we won't talk about it. Ah, poor Jill. She came here, you know. My son sent her. We had lovely chats. She wanted me to leave her that little desk over there in my will. But it's George II and I told her she couldn't have it because I am leaving everything to my son and she never came back. Sad."

"Did she tell you anything about herself?" asked Agatha.

"Oh, yes. She was married when she was living in Evesham. But she said he was a brute and threatened to kill her."

"Have you told the police this?"

"They didn't ask Jenny."

Agatha leaned forward. "Have you any idea where in Evesham she used to live and was her married name Davent?"

"She said the cinema was at the end of the street. Wait a bit. A tree. She was married to a tree. No, the house was called after a tree."

"Something like The Firs?" said Agatha, beginning to feel she had wandered into Looking-Glass country.

"What was it?" Jenny stared at the ceiling for inspiration. "Sycamore? Oak? Douglas, that's it. Like the Douglas fir."

A nurse appeared in the doorway. "Time for your exercises," she said. The nurse smiled at Agatha. "We like to keep our clients mobile."

"Will you come again?" asked Jenny.

"Certainly," said Agatha.

As they moved together out of the room, the nurse whispered to Agatha, "Check your belongings and make sure she hasn't taken anything." Agatha looked in her handbag.

"My wallet's missing!"

"Wait there. I know where she hides things."

The nurse returned with Agatha's wallet. Jenny was walking ahead down the corridor.

"I've got to catch her," said the nurse. "If I don't, she'll be back to the shops in Mircester, pinching things. See yourself out."

Agatha stopped at the reception desk. "I gather that Mrs. Harcourt is a kleptomaniac," she said to the male nurse.

"Fortunately, not all the time," he said. "She can go months until something excites her and then she raids the shops. But you're her relative. You must have known that."

"It's been kept very quiet," said Agatha. She was heading for the door when she stopped still. What if Jenny had stolen something from Jill and it was still in her room?

She turned around. The nurse had left the reception desk and was hurrying into the back regions. Agatha ran lightly up the stairs and located Jenny's room. When that nurse had gone back to get her wallet, she had gone to the desk. In the drawers of the desk were old photographs, scarves, and cheap jewellery. Grateful for all the programmes on antiques on television which showed where secret drawers were located in old desks, Agatha found one. Inside was a small black book. She snatched it up as she heard footsteps in the corridor outside. The footsteps went on past the door. Agatha ran down the stairs and out to her car and drove away as quickly as possible.

She stopped a little way from Sunnydale, parking in a space by a farm gate.

Agatha opened the book. Jill's name was on the inside front page. It was a sort of small ledger with lists of payments. The entries ranged from twenty to five hundred pounds. Beside each sum of money was only one initial and the dates of the payments. Agatha sighed. If, by a very long shot, this book belonged to Jill and was evidence of blackmail, then it followed that she should turn it over to the police so that they could match

77

it with any files they had taken from Jill's office or with anything on her computer.

But she could imagine the questions. "You *stole* this book, Mrs. Raisin. Did you inform Sunnydale you had taken it without a patient's knowledge?" And on and on it would go.

It must be Jill's, surely. It had her name on it. The payments stopped one day before her murder.

Were these single initials from first or last names? The twenty-pound payment was marked with the initial *V.* Could that be Victoria Bannister?

Agatha thirsted for revenge on Victoria. She decided to go to Carsely and confront the woman. Then she would decide what to do about the book.

Victoria was weeding in her front garden when Agatha opened the gate.

"What do you want?" Victoria demanded harshly.

"I wondered why you were paying Jill Davent blackmail to the sum of twenty pounds a month," said Agatha.

Victoria's face turned a muddy colour. "Nonsense!"

Agatha shrugged and held up the little book. "Just thought I'd give you a chance to explain before I turn this record over to the police."

Victoria slumped down onto the grass and buried her face in her hands.

"If you tell me and it's nothing really awful, I won't tell the police," said Agatha.

Victoria slowly got to her feet. "Do you mean that?"

"Depends what you did."

"Come inside. Someone might hear us."

The kitchen into which Victoria led Agatha was surprisingly welcoming and cheerful to belong to such an acidulous woman. There was a handsome Welsh dresser with Crown Derby plates and geraniums in tubs at the open window.

They both sat down at an oak table. "It's like this," said Victoria. "Do you remember Mrs. Cooper's dog?"

"The nasty little thing that yapped all the time?"

"She lives next door. I couldn't bear the noise anymore. I crushed up a lot of my sleeping pills and put them in a bowl of chopped steak. When the beast fell unconscious, I put it in a sack and drowned it in the rain barrel. Then I buried it."

"And how did Jill find out?"

"She seemed ever such a good listener, and no one ever listens to me. So I paid for a consultation. The death of that dog was on my conscience. So I told her. The next thing I know she was demanding regular payments for my silence. I had to pay up."

"You've confirmed for me that this was Jill's," said Agatha. "I won't tell the police. But why did Jill tell you about my background?"

"That was before I actually consulted her. We were having a drink and she told me."

"So why spread it around?"

She hung her head. "I don't know. I told the police about you threatening to kill her because I didn't want them to start looking at me."

"Just keep clear of me in the future," said Agatha. "You are a sickening woman."

As Agatha was about to enter her cottage, she was hailed by James Lacey, who hurried to join her. "Toni's just called me," he said. "She told me to look out for you as someone just tried to kill you."

"Come in and I'll tell you all about it. I haven't had lunch and I must eat something."

Agatha told him, between bites of a cheese sandwich, everything that had happened, ending up with, "So I think I'll have to throw myself on Bill's mercy, but first, I'd like to track down the husband."

"I'd better come with you."

Agatha looked at him. There he was, as handsome as ever from his lightly tanned face and bright blue eyes to his tall muscular figure. Why did she no longer feel a thing?

"Right," said Agatha. "Let's go. I'll drive."

As they turned into the road that led up the side of the Regal Cinema, Agatha said, "I'm glad they restored that old cinema. Must go one day. Now, I'll put the car in the parking place and we can start knocking on doors."

When Agatha parked the car and got a parking ticket, she returned to find James searching his iPad. "I'm just checking if there are any Davents in this street. Did she keep her married name?"

"Oh, Lord, I don't know," said Agatha crossly, cross because she had been caught out at missing a basic piece of detection.

"Oh, here we are," said James. "There's a T. Davent at number 905A. That must be right along at the end. The *A* probably means it's a basement flat, or what the estate agents call a garden flat."

"So it's not called Douglas. I wonder what she was talking about?"

"Who?

"Tell you later."

They started to walk. The day had turned hot and humid. Agatha felt uneasily that her make-up was melting and running down her neck.

"Don't take such long strides," she complained.

"You shouldn't wear such high heels the whole time," commented James. But he slowed his pace. He looked down at the top of Agatha's glossy hair and felt an odd pang of loss. But surely it was Agatha's fault that their marriage had not worked out. She would go on smoking and insisted on carrying on working. But what he missed was her old, unquestioning adoration of him.

"Here we are at last," said Agatha. "Of course, with my bloody luck, he'll be out working. Let's try the basement. Yes, the name on the door is Davent." She rang the bell.

The door was opened by a small, blond woman with a discontented face. Agatha guessed she was in her late thirties.

"I don't want encyclopaedias, I've got double glazing and I don't believe in God," she said harshly.

Agatha rapidly introduced herself. "I was hoping to talk to Mr. Davent."

"I'm his sister, Freda. If you want to ask him about the bitch from hell, you'll find him at his shop, Computing Plus, on the Four Pools estate."

"Did you know Jill Davent?" asked James.

"I don't want to talk about that cow. The day I heard about her murder was like Christmas. Now shove off."

The door slammed.

"Back to the car," said James, "and let's see exactly where we can find Computing Plus."

After circling around the Four Pools business estate, they found the shop, parked the car and walked in. The shop was full of expensive-looking equipment. One young man was serving a couple, while another leaned on the desk, reading a newspaper. Agatha approached the newspaper reader. "Is Mr. Davent available?"

"If it's a complaint, I can maybe deal with it," he said in a strong Eastern European accent. Probably Polish, thought Agatha. Evesham was rapidly becoming Little Poland.

Agatha handed him her card. "Tell him I would like to ask him a few questions."

The young man disappeared into a back office with a frosted-glass door. "Stop eyeing his bottom, Agatha," admonished James.

"It's those skintight black jeans," said Agatha ruefully. "They just scream, 'look at my bum.'"

"Be your age."

"No wonder our marriage didn't work out," snarled Agatha. "Always nitpicking and complaining. Furthermore . . ."

The office door opened. "You're to go in," said the assistant.

They walked in. Davent stood up to meet them. Agatha introduced herself and James.

"I don't know how I can help you," he said. "I have had so many grillings from the police."

"Just a few questions, Mr. Davent."

"Call me Tris. It's short for Tristram."

He was a good-looking man in possibly his early for-ties. He was of moderate height with a thick head of hair with auburn highlights. He was wearing a charcoal grey suit with a striped shirt and blue silk tie. He had neat regular features and a square chin with a dimple in it.

"Please sit down," he said. Tris sat behind his desk and Agatha and James took chairs in front of it.

"It's like this," said Agatha. "In order to find out who murdered your late wife, we have to know more about her background. Was she a therapist when you met her?"

"No, she was a tart."

"Why did you marry her?" asked James curiously.

He sighed. "I'll begin at the beginning. I went to a computer conference in Chicago, ten years ago. Jill was blond then. She just seemed to be one of the computer crowd. My wife had died of cancer the year before. Jill was a good listener. She was English and I was lonely. We ended up in bed together. In the morning, she said she had an important appointment and had to rush. We arranged to meet in the hotel bar that evening. That's when I found my wallet was missing."

"Did you tell the police?"

"I felt I had been conned. I was too ashamed. I still turned up in the bar that evening at the appointed time and wasn't much surprised when she didn't turn up. I put it down to experience. Two months later, she turned up at my address in Evesham in tears, saying she was pregnant. I accused her of stealing my wallet and she looked horrified. She denied the whole thing and said someone must have picked my pocket when we were in the bar. She said she was a qualified therapist. My late wife could not have children and I wanted to believe her. So we got married.

Then after four months, she said she'd had a miscarriage. I had begun to get suspicious of her. She was somehow so . . . how can I describe it? . . . glib.

One day when she was out, I searched her things. I found my wallet. No money, but the cards were there. I taxed her with it and she said that she had been unable to keep her appointment in the bar but had been so worried about the missing wallet that she had got hold of the hotel detective. The wallet had been found in the hotel trash. When I was in my shop, I phoned the hotel and asked to speak to the detective. He said no one had asked him to look for any wallet. He asked for Jill's name. I told him her maiden name was Jill Sommerville. He told me to phone him the following day, which I did. He said Jill had been working for a high-class escort agency and I had been well and truly conned. I confronted Jill again and said unless she agreed to an immediate and uncontested divorce, I would take her to court. She agreed. She moved out immediately. She was as cold as ice. She jeered at me and called me a boring fool. She said she had been tired of the life."

Agatha supressed a groan. Prostitution, however classy, often came with a package of drugs, crime and pimps. Someone could have followed her from America. It could even be some other man she had cheated. Agatha felt deflated and at a complete loss. She could not bring herself to believe that this ex-husband might be a murderer.

"Are you two an item?" asked Tris.

"We were married but it didn't work out," said Agatha.

Tris grinned. "Join the club."

Outraged, James got to his feet. "I will wait for you outside," he said coldly to Agatha, and stalked out.

"I shouldn't have said that. Should I go after him?" asked Tris.

"It's all right. He's miffed because it was a bit rude to compare your awful marriage to ours."

"Let me make it up to you?" said Tris. "What about dinner one night?"

"All right," said Agatha. Inside, a little Agatha was jumping around, yelling, "Yipee! I've still got pulling power."

"What about tomorrow night?" asked Tris.

"Where and when?" asked Agatha.

"Would you like to try Polish food? There's a good restaurant round the corner from where I live called Warsaw Home."

"Won't it be dumplings and red cabbage?"

"No, the menu's varied."

"I'll meet you there," said Agatha. What time?"

"Eight o'clock."

"You're on. I better go and soothe James down."

"I wouldn't trust that one as far as I could throw him," raged James. "Cheeky sod."

"He apologised very nicely," said Agatha.

"Has it crossed your tiny mind that he might be the murderer?"

"I don't think so," said Agatha. "We've forgotten about wolfsbane or monkshood. The Carsely gardens are open to the public on Saturday. Let's go round as many as we can and see if anyone is growing the stuff."

"You go," said James, folding his arms and staring out of the windscreen. "I have work to do. Are you seeing that chap again?"

"I shouldn't think so," lied Agatha. "I think he's told us the lot. I wish someone would pay me to find out the identity of the murderer because a trip to Chicago would be expensive."

Agatha dropped James and went to search out the soothing presence of her friend Mrs. Bloxby.

When she had finished telling Mrs. Bloxby all the latest news, the vicar's wife looked worried.

"I would almost feel relieved if the murderer were someone from Chicago," she said.

"Why?" demanded Agatha.

"I feel it must be someone Miss Davent was blackmailing."

"She's Mrs."

"Oh, well. Her. They are slimy sorts of murders. Someone from Chicago would not necessarily know about you. Are you going to take that blackmailing ledger to Detective Wong?"

"I suppose I must," said Agatha. "But I can't say I stole it from Jenny Harcourt's desk. I can't lie and say she gave it to me or they'll question her and she's not that daft. Certainly, she wouldn't have known it was there. For some reason, Jill picked on that as a good hiding place. She must have begun to feel threatened. I know, I'll say it was shoved through my letter box. Now, to try to get Bill on his own. But first, I'd better go home and copy out what's written in that book."

Chapter Five

Through Patrick Mulligan's contacts, Agatha found that Bill was due to finish his shift at seven that evening. Realising she was still very hungry, she stopped in at an all-day breakfast restaurant and demolished a plate of sausage, eggs, bacon and chips, all washed down with coffee. Then she managed to secure an appointment for a facial at a beauty parlour and feeling refreshed and newly made-up, she called in at the George Hotel bar for a double gin and tonic before finally taking up a position in the car park opposite police headquarters, where she could watch for Bill coming out.

At last she saw him emerging and called to him. "Get in the car," ordered Agatha. "I've got something to show you."

"What have you been up to now?" asked Bill.

"This came through my letter box," said Agatha. She had carefully wiped the book free of prints other than her own, because she thought that they might have Jenny Harcourt's fingerprints on file, as the woman was a kleptomaniac. Agatha suddenly wondered if Jill had hidden the book in that desk or if Jenny had stolen it.

"What do you think it is?" asked Bill.

"It looks to me of a record of blackmailing payments," said Agatha. "There is only one initial at each payment."

Bill had that sixth sense that a few good detectives are blessed with and he was suddenly sure that Agatha had not just received the book through her letter box.

"You'd better come back to the station with me and make a statement," he said. "Are you telling me the truth? This really did come through your letter box?"

"Would I lie to you?"

"Yes."

"Oh, Bill. Wilkes will get in on the act and he'll bully me."

"He's off duty. Come along."

———

As Bill carefully took down Agatha's statement, he seemed to turn from friend to efficient detective. When exactly had she found the book? Why had she taken so long to contact the police? She should have phoned right away.

Exasperated, Agatha complained, "I wanted to tell you! Right! I did not want Wilkes accusing me of murder or interfering in a police investigation." At last the ledger was bagged up and she was free to leave. "Coming for a drink?" she asked.

"No," said Bill. "I'll need to get onto this right away, and, sorry, but I'll need to contact Wilkes at home."

"Did you find out who sent me that poisonous bouquet?"

"Yes. One of the market traders said he found the flowers on his stall with a letter and a fifty-pound note asking him to deliver it to you. He didn't want to leave his stall, so he gave that little boy the bouquet to take to your office. Just think, Agatha. If he hadn't been so honest, he could have pocketed the money and taken the flowers home to his wife."

When Agatha parked outside her cottage, James came hurrying to meet her. "There's something you should know," he said.

"What?"

"I think Davent gets highlights put in his hair and that dimple on his chin, I'll bet, was put there by a cosmetic surgeon."

"So what?" demanded Agatha. "I've just had a facial."

"It's different for men. He's probably gay."

"If he's gay, why has he asked me out on a date?"

"Probably to bump you off, you silly woman."

"Oh, go and take a running jump, you tiresome bore."

James swung round and stomped off.

Agatha was just about to unlock her door, when a car bearing Wilkes and Bill drove up, followed by a forensic unit. Agatha groaned. Of course, they would want to check her door for fingerprints.

"Get in the car," ordered Wilkes. "We've got to let the forensic boys do their stuff."

"No," said Agatha. "I don't want to sit in a stuffy car. You can interview me in the pub."

It was a warm, humid evening. They sat at a table in the pub garden, away from the other drinkers.

To Agatha's relief, Wilkes was less suspicious than Bill. But while she talked, Agatha was aware of Bill's almond-shaped eyes fastened on her face, those beautiful eyes he had inherited from his Chinese father. Bill Wong had been her first friend after she had moved to the Cotswolds. Agatha was very fond of the young detective and hated lying to him. The tape recorder on the table recorded everything Agatha said.

Victoria Bannister watched the group through the pub window. From her vantage point, it looked to her as if Agatha were being treated with great respect. She felt a sudden surge of jealousy. The fact that Agatha had promised to keep her name from the police did not seem to count. She was bitterly jealous. She had staked out Jill's consulting room, watching her clients, trying and failing to summon up courage to plead with Jill to stop blackmailing her. Surely, she had not been the only one blackmailed. But she did not want to find herself in the clutches of a murderer. She did not trust Agatha to keep her name from the police. Victoria suddenly decided that she needed company in her misery. Perhaps if she followed the last likely person she had seen visiting Jill and had followed them home, she might get help.

Although Agatha kept busy the following day and looked forward to her date with Tris, she found she was nervous. Somewhere out there was a murderer trying to kill her. The first attempt had failed but surely the murderer would try again. Usually, she would have fretted about what to wear for her date, but fear of a lurking murderer made her concentrate on her work to try to banish fear.

She got into her car after work and reversed into a lamppost. Cursing, she got out. There wasn't much damage. Taking a deep breath, she drove carefully to Evesham, looking all the while in the rearview mirror in case she was being followed. A man driving a BMW appeared to be tailing her closely. Agatha swung into a lay-by and waited but the BMW drove on. She suddenly wanted to forget about her date and get home to the security of her cottage, well protected by burglar alarms. She missed her cats. Although they often seemed indifferent to her, there had been occasions when, sensing her distress, they had followed her up to bed and snuggled down beside her. And where was faithless Charles?

At that moment, Charles, who had called on Agatha, and, finding her not at home, knocked on James's door and asked if he knew where Agatha had gone.

James let off a diatribe about Agatha's morals. He ended with, "And I don't believe her when she says it isn't a date. Just detecting."

"Might check it out," said Charles. "Where does this Davent live?"

"You'd better order for me," said Agatha after a look at the menu. "All this is new to me."

He signalled the waitress and ordered two vodkas. "This'll be my limit," said Agatha. "I don't want to be charged with drink driving."

"By the time you've got through this meal," said Tris, "you'll be as sober as anything. The food really mops the alcohol up."

He ordered a thick mushroom soup to start and then to follow, bigos, a "hunter" stew full of various types of meat and sausages, cooked in sauerkraut, and a pile of potato pancakes. He wanted to order beer, but Agatha said she detested the stuff so he ordered more vodka. They talked idly of this and that, about the decline of the centre of Evesham and what had caused the death of the high streets of Britain, Agatha being lulled by the heavy food and the vodka. When he ordered yet more vodka, she didn't protest. Agatha was tired of feeling frightened. And he was an attractive man. He couldn't be gay. He'd been married. She fought down the voice in her head reminding her of gays she had known who were married. And did it matter a damn anyway? It was not as if she was going to spend the night with him. She began to talk about the murders and how an attempt had been made on her life.

Over the dessert of huge slices of cheesecake, he leaned across the table and took her hand. "You're a very attractive woman, Agatha. I wish you would drop this case."

"Why?"

"It's too dangerous. Just drop it."

He was staring into her eyes and his grip on her hand tightened. His voice had held a note of command.

Agatha could feel the euphoria induced by vodka and heavy food fading away. She tried to pull her hand away, but he held on to it.

"Promise me," he said. "I am sure if you go on with this investigation, something really nasty could happen to you. He's already tried to kill you with wolfsbane."

Agatha jerked her hand savagely away with such force that a glass went flying. "How did you know it was wolfsbane?" she asked. "That wasn't in the newspapers."

"It stands to reason. Herythe was killed with wolfs-bane."

"But Jill was strangled and Clive Tremund was clubbed and drowned."

"Don't get mad at me," pleaded Tris. "It was an educated guess. It was—"

"Hullo, darling. Not watching your waistline again?"

"Oh, Charles," said Agatha weakly. "What are you doing here?"

"Came to find you. The police want to talk to you again, so I thought I'd come and hold your hand. Maybe I'd better drive you. Been swilling the vodka, have you?"

Agatha made the introductions. "I'd better go," she said to Tris.

"When will I see you again?" he asked.

"I'll phone you," said Agatha.

"How on earth did you find me?" asked Agatha, as they walked to Charles's car.

"James told me about your interviewing Tristram Davent and knowing your predilection for unsuitable men, I went to the address James gave me and his sister told me where you were. Leave your car. I'll take you to pick it up in the morning."

When Agatha was seated in the passenger seat, Charles turned to her and asked curiously, "Why aren't you livid with me for breaking up your date with fancy pants back there?"

"Drive on. He has to pass the car park to get to his home. I don't want to see him again."

"Okay." Charles left the car park and swung round onto Port Street.

"It's like this," said Agatha. She told him what had happened in the restaurant. "It wasn't just what he said," she explained. "I've been a bag of nerves since the attempt on my life and he actually scared me."

"Why on earth did you agree to a date with him?"

"I'm a detective! Remember!" howled Agatha. "I thought he might come up with some more interesting information on Jill."

"Be honest, Aggie. He asked you for a date and you jumped at it. Raise your standards. A man with highlights in his hair."

"It could be natural."

"Rubbish."

A tear ran down Agatha's cheek. "J-just take me home and b-bugger off," she sobbed.

Charles swung into a lay-by and switched off the engine.

"I didn't mean to be so rude. Don't cry. I've never seen you so rattled before. Cheer up. We'll go to your cottage, have a drink and watch something silly on television. I know you won't give up. So what's your next move?"

Agatha dried her eyes and sniffed loudly. "I'm going round the Carsely gardens tomorrow. They're open to the public. I want to see if anyone's got wolfsbane."

"If they had the stuff, they've probably uprooted it by now. Don't worry. I'll come with you. Do you know how to recognise it?"

"I've Googled lots of photos. It's sometimes called monkshood and the poison is aconite."

"Right. We're on for tomorrow. But I do think you should tell Bill about your dinner. I mean, the man was threatening."

"Maybe," said Agatha, but feeling she could not bear another questioning as to why she had agreed to have dinner with Davent. She was only in her early fifties. But had she fallen so low, she wondered, that she would consider any man who asked her out attractive?

The following day, when they set out to tour the gardens, was sunny. Great fleecy clouds were tugged like galleons across a large blue Cotswold sky by a light breeze. "Not all the gardens are open to the public, surely," said Charles.

"We'll pretend we don't know. I hope this isn't a complete waste of time. Someone Jill got on the wrong side of in America could have followed her over."

"Then," said Charles, "one would think that person, having murdered her, would clear off back to the States. Okay. There's Tremund. But whoever our murderer is, he might have thought Tremund had dug up something. But what about Herythe and the attempt on your life? That suggests someone closer to home."

"Let's try Victoria Bannister first," said Agatha. "Now, she *is* deranged."

"Is her garden open?"

"Don't know. We'll pretend it is."

They made their way along the cobbled streets of the village, up past the vicarage to where Victoria lived.

"Not many people about," commented Charles. "Is it always this quiet when it is open gardens day?"

"Probably," said Agatha. "Mrs. Bloxby once said that they are so jealous in the village that at the beginning of the day they often don't want to visit anyone else's garden. Then they all turn out."

"Aren't you worried that Victoria will start screaming insults at you?" asked Charles.

"No, she got a shock when I threatened to sue her for libel."

"She hasn't got a 'Garden's Open' sign up on her gate," Charles pointed out.

"So what?" demanded Agatha, pushing the gate open.

The little front garden of the thatched cottage was crammed with flowers. Tall hollyhocks raised their blossoms to the summer sky. White rambling roses tumbled round the low front door.

Agatha stopped suddenly on the path and Charles bumped into her. "Look!" whispered Agatha. "Wolfsbane!"

"You need to study those photos," said Charles. "That's a delphinium."

"Rats! I should have known it would be too easy."

Agatha rang the bell. "She must be out," she said, after they had waited a few minutes. "I know, let's go round to the garden at the back. If she comes home and catches us, we can lie and say we thought hers was one of the open gardens."

But when they arrived in the back garden, it showed that the flower display was all at the front. There was a shaggy lawn dominated by a clothesline. At the end of the garden was a shed. Along the back fence were two crab apple trees.

"Let's have a look in the shed," said Agatha.

"She might catch us."

"Don't be a wimp. Come on."

"No," said Charles firmly. "You see that garden chair up by the house? I'm going to sit on that until you are finished. If I hear her coming, I'm running away."

"Boneless creep!" Agatha made her way down the garden. Three large crows that had been pecking at something flew up at her approach.

Outside the shed, what at first looked like a bundle of clothes lay on the ground. Curious, Agatha moved forward. Then she let out a high-pitched scream that brought Charles running to her side.

The dead eyeless face of Victoria Bannister stared up at them. "The crows," babbled Agatha. "They've pecked her eyes out!"

Charles put an arm round her. "Come away. We'll call the police. Come on, Aggie. Back away carefully or we'll be charged with mucking up the crime scene."

The police arrived. Agatha and Charles were taken outside the house to wait in a police car while the pathologist and Scenes of Crimes Operatives got to work.

Wilkes turned up and rapped on the window of the car in which Agatha and Charles were sitting. "We'll move down to your cottage, Mrs. Raisin," he said, "and take your statements there."

Why is it so sunny? wondered Agatha bleakly. It ought to be dark and gloomy. The village looks so normal. Unaware yet of the drama, some villagers had started to trot in and out of the gardens.

At her cottage, Agatha insisted they move into the garden, where she could smoke. Wilkes was accompanied by Bill Wong, Alice Peterson and a policewoman.

"I'm amazed you are still indulging in that filthy habit," commented Wilkes.

"A woman has been found dead with her eyes pecked out by crows and all you can do is bitch about my smoking," said Agatha. "Get on with it."

They crowded round Agatha's garden table and the questioning began. When the grilling came to an end, Agatha told them about her dinner with Tris Davent, saying, "He scared me. I'll bet he did it."

"Wait a minute," said Wilkes. "I've got to make a phone call."

He moved off into the kitchen. "Are you all right, Agatha?" asked Bill. "You look quite white."

"I'm shaky," said Agatha. "It was really nasty."

Wilkes came back. "The first estimate of the time of death from the liver temperature is yesterday evening, maybe between seven and midnight. The coroner will have a better idea when he checks the content of her stomach. It can't be Davent. You're his alibi, Mrs. Raisin."

"Not necessarily," said Agatha stubbornly. "I left the restaurant at nine-thirty. He would have time to get to Carsely and bump her off."

"Highly unlikely," said Wilkes sourly. "Now, you, Sir Charles Fraith. We'll now have your version of events."

Agatha envied the calm way Charles talked. He looked just as if finding a gruesome murdered body was a normal event. She had nearly gone to his bed the night before, stopping herself just in time, reminding herself that casual sex was out. But she had longed to be held and comforted. Neither James nor Charles were exactly affectionate, she thought. James was more of the "wham, bam, thank you, ma'am" type of lover. Charles was expert and yet when it was all over, he remained as much of an enigma as ever, never betraying what he really thought of her. She closed her eyes against the glare of the sun and went off into a dream of a steady, dependable man. He would have a rugged face and wear tweeds. He would potter about the garden and in the winter's evenings, they would sit by the fire. He would be passionate and loving in bed. He—

"You've gone quite red, Aggie," said Charles.

"It's the sun," said Agatha, opening her eyes and looking at the beautifully dressed and barbered figure that was Charles.

The doorbell rang. "I'll get it," said Alice.

She returned, followed by Toni, Simon and James.

"James phoned us," said Toni. "How awful, Agatha. Are you all right?"

"Surviving," said Agatha. "We'd better move indoors. There isn't enough room here."

"We're off," said Wilkes. "Report to headquarters later today and sign your statements. And don't speak to the press!"

James, Simon and Toni settled themselves in the garden chairs vacated by the police and demanded to know what on earth had been happening. James said the news of Victoria's death had gone round the village, thanks to a policeman on duty who had been found gossiping.

Agatha wearily went over the whole thing again, including her dinner with Davent. She had just finished when there came a furious ringing at the doorbell.

"I'll go," said Toni.

"Look through the spy hole and if it's the press, don't open the door."

When Toni came back, she said ruefully, "If you wonder why the ringing has stopped, Agatha, your friend Roy Silver is on your doorstep, holding forth."

Agatha groaned. "James, be a darling and go and open the door and jerk him inside."

Roy Silver had once worked for Agatha when she had run her public relations business.

James returned with a sheepish-looking Roy. To Agatha's horror, the young man seemed to be covered in tattoos. "What a mess you've made of yourself," she said. "Do you know that when that fad dies, you'll be left with a large bill for cosmetic surgery to get all that removed?"

They all stared at the spider decorating his neck and the swirling multicoloured tattoos of snakes up his arms. "It washes off," said Roy sulkily. "It's the thing. I'm doing PR for this boy band, Hell on Earth. They're going to be big."

"What did you say to the press?" demanded Agatha. "I've been warned not to talk to them."

"I simply told them the truth," said Roy moodily. "I said I had helped you with cases before and I was helping you with this one."

"How did you know about this one?" asked Toni.

"I didn't. But the reporters told me there had been a murder in the village, so I winged it."

Agatha looked sourly at his weak face and gelled hair, and at his jeans carefully torn at the knees, and said, "You look as if you've crawled out of a young offenders' institute. Go upstairs and wash that muck off, or you're not staying!"

"That's the trouble with you burying yourself in Peasantville," said Roy. "You're no longer trendy. Oh, I'm going."

"I think," said Toni, "that now we are here, Simon and I should do a tour of the gardens and see if we can find that wretched flower anywhere. We can split up and—"

"Go together," said Agatha. "I don't want either of you getting killed."

Chapter Six

"Are you sure we shouldn't split up?" asked Toni uneasily. Simon had been relentlessly pursuing her for a long time.

Simon's jester's face crinkled up in a smile. "Relax. I'm spoken for."

"Who? What's happened?"

"I'm engaged," said Simon triumphantly.

"Who is she?"

"Detective Sergeant Ruby Carson."

"The one from Oxford?"

"That's her. I can't believe my luck. I finally got her

out on a date last night. I said, joking, you know, 'Marry me!' And she said, 'Yes.'"

"Was she serious?"

"Yes. I'm going to meet her children tonight."

"Children? Is she divorced?"

"Yes, she's got two kids, Pearl, who's five, and Jonathan, nine."

Toni looked at him uneasily. "How old is she?"

"Early forties."

"You're early twenties, Simon. Oh, please don't rush into things."

"I'm in love," said Simon stubbornly. "If you're going to be nasty about it, I don't want to talk about it anymore. Let's look for this damned plant."

"You know," said Toni slowly, "before we start here, what about running over to Ancombe and having a look at Gwen Simple's garden? I think, because Agatha can't ever get anywhere with her, she's forgotten that she should really be our prime suspect."

As Toni drove the short distance to Ancombe, she worried about Simon. Agatha was bad enough, falling into obsession with one man or another, but surely Simon was just as bad. He had claimed to love her more than anyone in the world before he joined the army and left for Afghanistan, only to return engaged to a female sergeant, whom he then ditched at the altar, and then had begun to pursue her again. Like Agatha, there was something not quite emotionally grown up about Simon.

She could not imagine Simon as a stepfather. She remembered Ruby Carson to be, yes, beautiful, but highly efficient and, Toni was sure, highly ambitious.

At that very moment, Chief Superintendent Alistair White was admiring Ruby's naked curves as she climbed out of bed. "I'd better collect the children from Mum," she said. "Oh, I won't be seeing you for a while."

"Why? Nobody knows about us."

"I know. But I'm engaged."

"You're what! Who to?"

"A young fellow called Simon Black who works for Agatha Raisin."

"Why on earth . . . ?"

Ruby came back and sat on the edge of the bed. "He works for that Raisin agency and that bloody woman has solved more cases than I've had hot dinners. Young Simon will keep me in the loop as to what she's found out. Then goodbye. But in the meantime, we'll cool it. Anyway, God forbid your missus should find out."

"You're a hard woman, Sergeant."

Ruby grinned. "Now, inspector sounds so much nicer, doesn't it?"

Gwen Simple lived in a bungalow in the shadow of the church in Ancombe.

"Oh, good," said Toni, as they got out of the car. "She's got a 'Gardens Open' sticker on her gate. They must be having an open day as well."

"She'll think we're still chasing her," said Simon.

"Too bad," said Toni. "There are a good few people in her garden. Can't see her. Come along." Toni gave him a coloured photograph of wolfsbane.

"Is it wolfsbane or monkshood?" asked Simon.

"Two names for the same plant," said Toni. "I prefer wolfsbane. Sounds more murderous." Her phone rang. She pulled it out of the pocket of her shorts. Simon heard her say, "Hullo, Agatha. What? Are you sure? Do you believe that?"

When she had rung off, she said, "It seems as if Victoria Bannister is the murderer, or so the police believe."

"Why on earth do they think that?"

"When they pried open her dead hands, she was clutching wolfsbane. And she left a note, saying the death had been on her conscience. They found two plants in her shed with a lot of the leaves torn off."

"I don't believe it," said Simon. "It's a nasty death."

"Agatha says she confessed to killing her neighbour's

dog. What if someone knew about that?" said Toni. "A village lady such as Victoria would not be able to face the shame. And she said 'murder,' not 'murders.' Can you imagine Victoria even killing Tremund and dumping him in the river? It's ridiculous. But, believe me, the police have been under a lot of pressure from the media. They won't want any other solution. Oh, there's Gwen in the doorway. Let's look at her garden anyway."

Gwen still looked as if she had stepped down from a mediaeval painting from her dead-white face, long nose and thick eyelids shielding brown eyes. She was wearing a long silk summer gown in a swirling pattern of green and gold.

She stood very still, watching them as they entered the garden and made their way from plant to plant to bush to flower.

"Gwen gives me the creeps," whispered Simon, "but she wouldn't have the strength, say, to murder Tremund."

"That one could charm a man into doing it for her," said Toni.

Gwen had moved into the garden and was speaking to a large muscular man.

He approached Toni and Simon and growled, "Get lost. Mrs. Simple has had enough of you detectives making her life a misery. Get out or I'll throw you out!"

"See what I mean?" said Toni when they had beaten a retreat.

As Roy Silver sat in Agatha's living room that evening, desperately switching from news channel to news channel in the hope of seeing himself talking to the press and failing to find anything, Simon was arriving at Ruby's house in Oxford.

He had an engagement ring in his pocket and was clutching a large bouquet of roses.

Ruby answered the door but turned her face away to avoid a kiss. "I've heard the news," she said curtly. "Case solved. This is not a good evening, Simon. I've had a hard day and I'm pretty tired. Can we take a rain check?"

"The case isn't solved by a long shot," said Simon, looking hurt and disappointed. Two children appeared behind Ruby and stared at him with flat eyes.

"What? Come in, sit down," said Ruby, suddenly smiling. "What do you mean it's not solved?"

She led him into the kitchen. Simon, although she had originally invited him for dinner, noticed gloomily that there were no signs of cooking.

The boy, Jonathan, said, "Have you brought us presents?"

"Sorry," said Simon.

"Go and watch television," ordered Ruby. "You can have half an hour before bed."

They trailed off. "Now," said Ruby eagerly. "What's all this?"

Simon told her about Victoria killing the neighbour's dog and said that Agatha was sure someone had threatened to expose her, left her the wolfsbane, and Victoria had committed suicide or that she had been forced into leaving the note.

Ruby rose from the kitchen table and came back with a notebook and began to write busily. Simon felt he was back in the interrogation room as she asked question after question. At last she leaned back in her chair and smiled. "Is Agatha Raisin really clever?"

"Well, sometimes you wouldn't think so. But she blunders about, never giving up and she's got the most marvellous intuition."

"We've still got the outstanding murders of Tremund and Herythe," said Ruby. "Any chance of an introduction to your boss?"

"Yes, of course."

"What about now?"

"What about our dinner?"

"That can wait." She leaned forward and gave Simon a lingering kiss on the lips. "Phone her."

Agatha said she would like to meet Ruby. Charles had left and Roy was moaning about his lack of publicity.

Ruby took her children round to her mother's, but before they set off in Ruby's car, Simon said awkwardly, "I wouldn't mention anything to Agatha about us being an item. She can be controlling."

"Don't worry. Won't say a word."

"We met before," said Agatha to Ruby. "Simon tells me you are still interested in the murders. Come in. This is a friend of mine, Roy Silver. Roy, Detective Sergeant Ruby Carson."

"Any press in the village?" asked Roy.

"Couldn't see any," said Ruby. "If there are any, they'll be hanging around the Bannister woman's cottage."

"I think I'll get some fresh air," said Roy, heading for the door.

After he had gone, Agatha suggested they should sit in the garden because the evening was fine.

Over drinks, Ruby began to question Agatha. And when Agatha answered her questions, her curious bear-like eyes moved from Ruby's face to Simon's adoring one. Oh, dear, thought Agatha, I do believe she's using him and now me as well. Still, information works both ways. She could come in handy. But what's with young Simon? He looks well and truly smitten.

"There is the matter of Gwen Simple," said Agatha. "I could never believe she was innocent of the murders

114

her son committed. For some reason, men go weak at the knees when they come across her. I think she uses people, and if there is one thing I cannot bear, it is women who use sex to further their own ends. Don't you feel the same?"

"Of course," said Ruby, suddenly taking an intense dislike to Agatha.

"Are you married?" asked Agatha.

"Divorced."

"Children?"

"Two. Look, thank you for a most interesting talk but I'd better be getting back. Come along, Simon."

Simon was silent on the road back to Oxford. He was also hungry and bewildered. Agatha and Ruby had somehow made him feel like a small boy caught between two domineering aunts. The ring was in his pocket. But he was damned if he would give it to Ruby until there was a more romantic time.

Outside her house, Ruby looked at his worried face and said, "My darling, I am treating you horribly. Let Ruby make it up to you."

Simon could only be glad that because of the humidity of the evening and the sexual athletics in the front seat, the windows soon became steamed up.

After it was over and Ruby gave him a final kiss

goodnight, he got into his own car, wondering why he felt like a small boy who had failed his exams and had been given an apple by a sympathetic teacher.

Agatha sleepily answered the door, after peering through the spy hole, to survey a miserable-looking Simon. In the light of the lamp over the door, her sharp eyes took in his rumpled hair, swollen lips and love-bitten neck.

"Need a drink?" she asked, leading the way to the kitchen.

"I need food," said Simon.

"I'm not the world's greatest cook," said Agatha.

"Have you eggs?"

"Yes. Loads."

"Give me a pan and some butter and I'll make an omelette."

With rare forbearance, Agatha waited until he was fed. Then she said cautiously, "You look used."

"That's it," said Simon. He told her what had happened, ending up with, "I feel awful. In her car, in front of her house! What if the children had looked out of the window? What if Granny had brought them back? I've got a ring, Agatha. I meant to ask her to marry me."

"Take it back to the shop," said Agatha, stifling a yawn.

"Maybe she really does love me," said Simon plaintively. "Maybe I'm being too uptight about it all."

"The woman invites you for dinner," said Agatha patiently. "Instead, she uses you to come and grill me. She then gives you a quickie to keep you on the leash. That one is walking, talking ambition. Why don't you use her? We need good police contacts. Did they contact any of the people going into Tremund's office? Is there CCTV in that street?"

"Okay." Simon visibly brightened. He had been feeling hunted. Now he could play the role of the hunter.

"What do you feel about her now?" asked Agatha.

"I'm still in shock."

"Couldn't you just have held her off and suggested a bed would be a better place?"

"She was all over me. I thought we would move out of the car and into the house. I didn't expect to be dismissed."

"Did you use any protection?"

"Ruby had it with her."

"Cheer up," said Agatha. "She's got what she wants for now. But she'll be back."

"Another subject," said Simon. "Toni and I went over to Gwen's. We felt you had forgotten about her for the moment. We tried to look round her garden but a man chased us off."

The doorbell rang. "That'll be Roy back from a publicity hunt," said Agatha.

As she opened the door to him, she saw, over his shoulder, Charles arriving.

"Does nobody want to go to sleep?" complained Agatha.

"I'm off to London," said Roy sulkily. "I'll get my bag."

"What brings you?" Agatha asked Charles.

"I got a call from Adrian Sommerville. He says I can pick up the keys tomorrow and have a look at Jill's house. After we've had a look, we should call on him again, Agatha. I mean, did he know his sister was hooking in Chicago? What's her background? What does he think of her ex?"

"I'm tired," said Agatha. "I'll see you in the morning."

The day was humid and overcast. They collected the keys from an estate agent in Mircester, saying they did not need anyone to show them over, and then went back to Jill's cottage in Carsely.

The front garden looked even more neglected than the last time Agatha had seen it. Bits of yellow police tape fluttered amongst the bushes. Down in the village, the church bells rang out. Then came the tenor bell, and then the silence of a country Sunday.

"Here goes," said Charles, unlocking the door.

"You'd think that brother would have cleaned the place up," complained Agatha. "I'm surprised the estate agent didn't suggest it. There's still fingerprint dust everywhere."

"Let's start with the office," said Charles.

"You do that. I'll try the other rooms," said Agatha.

Across from the consulting room, on the other side of the small dark entrance hall, was a living room–cum–dining room. There were the usual things to be expected: television, bookcase, small table with four chairs, sofa and two armchairs, but no desk or chest of drawers. Agatha wondered whether to search through the books, but decided to leave them until later.

The kitchen was in the back. There were signs that the police had been through every food container. Agatha then made her way up the narrow wooden staircase. On the left of the landing was a bathroom. The cupboard over the hand basin was empty. No doubt the police had taken everything away. In the middle was a bedroom. There were no clothes or underwear. No doubt her brother had got rid of them. So no hope of finding anything in pockets. There was one room left, with a massage table and anatomical charts on the wall.

Agatha began to feel wearily that it was all a waste of time. The police would have been thorough in their search. There were three sockets in the house for hands-free phones but the phones were missing.

She trailed back down to the office. "Anything?" she asked Charles.

"Not a thing. Not even a phone," said Charles. "It's only in books where the detective finds something taped to the bottom of a drawer."

"Let's try the back garden," said Agatha. "With all her blackmailing carry-on, she must have needed places to hide things. I wonder if she hid that book in Jenny's desk or if kleptomaniac Jenny pinched it."

They walked through the kitchen to the back door. Charles tried several keys and then unlocked the door.

"She was no gardener," he said. The back garden was nothing but a square of weeds with a shed at the end. The day had turned very dark and as they made their way to the shed, lightning split the sky, followed by a massive crack of thunder.

Then the heavens opened and the rain came pouring down. The shed was unlocked. They dived into it out of the rain.

"Wasn't it Charles the Second who said that the English summer consisted of two days heat followed by a thunderstorm?" asked Charles.

Agatha scowled at him. She hated quotations. They made her feel more badly educated than she actually was. She looked around. Rusty garden implements were propped against the walls.

"I don't like this shed," said Agatha. "There's something wrong here."

"What?"

"I don't know."

"It's the storm," said Charles. "There's nothing here but us."

"Would she have buried things?" asked Agatha. "I mean, she thieved Tris's wallet and kept it. Perhaps she kept souvenirs of all the people she had conned. Maybe there's a loose plank or something."

"The floor looks untouched," said Charles. "There's nothing here."

"The police didn't dig up the garden," said Agatha, looking out of the grimy shed window.

"Why should they?" remarked Charles. "They weren't looking for dead bodies. I mean, Jill *was* the dead body. Look at it. That garden hasn't been touched in years."

"Snakes and bastards!" howled Agatha. "I'm sick of the whole thing."

"Never mind," said Charles. "The rain's easing off. Let's make a dash for it."

Agatha stumbled across the garden in her high-heeled sandals. One foot caught in the now muddy earth in front of shallow wooden steps leading up to the kitchen and she fell heavily.

Charles rushed to heave her up. "Look!" said Agatha.

There were three wide wooden steps and the top of one of them had become dislodged in her fall.

"There's something in there," she said excitedly. "It's a box."

"Put on gloves," said Charles.

Agatha pulled a pair of latex gloves out of her handbag. She lifted out a metal box. "I'll take it into the kitchen," she said.

She put it on the kitchen table. "It's not all that heavy. Let's see what we've got."

She took out items and laid them on the table. "We've two Rolex Oyster watches, three wallets, a big pile of notes, all sorts of currencies, sexy photographs of her in bed with various men. She must have had a partner to take these photos. What a contortionist she was! But no documents or letters."

"Anything in the wallets?"

"No cards. But family pictures in two of them."

"You'll need to call the police," said Charles.

"Do I have to?" wailed Agatha. "I found it."

"Agatha, those photos are probably from her hooking days in Chicago. You need the police to follow it up. That way, they'll find out who she was working with."

"Anybody home?" called a voice. Agatha put the items back in the box and slammed down the lid. "Who's there?"

"Me," said Simon, walking into the kitchen. "What have you got there?" He had been searching for her.

"Just found it," said Agatha. "I stumbled over a box of Jill's stuff. I'll need to call the police. There are photos she probably used to blackmail her clients in America."

"May I have a look?" asked Simon.

Agatha took the lid off the box again. "Hurry up. I'll phone Bill."

Simon carefully examined the items, his thoughts always on Ruby. He wanted the old Ruby back, the one he had been in love with. He had tried to call her that morning, but his calls went straight to her voice answering message. He knew if he left her a message about this discovery she would call him back, and he wanted to find out that the hard woman he had encountered the night before had changed back into the Ruby he wanted to marry.

"I really don't feel like waiting for the police, Agatha," said Simon. "I'm still upset about Ruby. Do you mind if I clear off?"

Chapter Seven

Simon walked down through the village to where he had left his car outside Agatha's cottage. He took out his mobile phone and dialled Ruby's number. It went straight to voice mail. "We've made a big discovery at Jill's cottage," said Simon. "If you want to hear about it, call me back."

He leaned against his car and waited. A sudden brisk breeze rustled through the leaves of the lilac tree outside Agatha's garden.

Simon felt a sudden frisson of fear. It was as if the leaves were whispering a warning. He looked along the lane. Nothing and nobody, except a discarded sweet wrapper that skittered along and stuck to his trousers.

His phone rang, making him jump. "Hullo, darling boy," cooed Ruby. "What have you got for me?"

"It's a terrific find," said Simon. "I'd rather see you in person."

"Come over. It's my day off," said Ruby.

When she rang off, she turned to her children. "I'm taking you to Granny."

"Wicked!" cried her son, Jonathan.

And Pearl said, "We love Granny more'n you."

Ruby shrugged and phoned her mother, who lived a few streets away. She fought down a small twinge of guilt. Her children spent more time with their grandmother than they ever did with her.

Simon drove to Oxford, praying that his dream of a warm and loving Ruby could be restored. He was about to ring the doorbell when he heard a man's voice through the open window of the living room, saying, "Don't you think I should stay? We're desperate for a break in this case."

"No, run along," came Ruby's voice. "The little sap is spoony about me and he might get jealous if he saw you and clam up."

"*I* might get jealous," said the man with a laugh.

"Don't be an idiot. He's just a rather boring little boy."

Simon backed off and crouched down behind a bush. The door opened and a thickset man came out. He kissed Ruby and walked off down the path.

The door closed and there was only the sound of the strengthening wind rustling through the leaves.

Simon suddenly felt immeasurably tired, silly and depressed. He crept out from behind the bush, making sure he was not observed from the windows of Ruby's house and made his way to his car and drove off. By the time he got back to Mircester, his phone had rung several times. Each time he recognised Ruby's number and finally switched his phone off.

Ruby paced angrily up and down her living room, wondering what to do. She tried to remind herself that if there was anything pertaining to the murder of Tremund, it would surely come through to Thames Valley Police and all she had to do was wait.

But she was ambitious and impatient. Simon had given her his address. She decided to drive to Mircester and challenge him.

The night was very dark. The air was sticky and humid and from far away came a rumble of thunder.

Her old car did not have air-conditioning and she was tired and sweating by the time she reached Simon's flat. Ruby rang the bell. But Simon, looking through the spy hole in his door, decided not to answer it. "The hell with her," he muttered, and went back to bed.

Frustrated and angry, Ruby decided to drive on to Carsely and confront Agatha Raisin.

Simon's flat was in a pedestrian area and so Ruby had left her car in the main square. Before she reached it, the heavens opened and the rain came pouring down. A flash of lightning lit up the square and she saw to her dismay that the back window of her car had been smashed. She slid into the front seat and tried to dry her sopping hair with some tissues. Police headquarters were beside the square but she decided against going in to report the window; they would consider that she was poaching on their territory. She noticed the streetlights were out. The storm must have caused a power cut.

Wearily, Ruby decided to forget about the whole thing and go home.

She was just about to switch on the engine when a wire was slid around her neck and viciously pulled tight. Ruby was a strong woman and tried to get her fingers under the wire without success. With one dying hand, she punched the hazard warning lights before everything turned black.

Bill Wong put up his umbrella as he left headquarters. Agatha Raisin had been released an hour before, after what Bill considered a merciless grilling from Wilkes, who seemed to persist in thinking that Agatha was impeding police enquiries.

As he made his way to his car, the rain suddenly switched off, as if some Olympian god had turned off a tap. Behind him he could hear the rumble of the police generator as it coped with the power cut.

He saw a car with flashing hazard lights and approached it curiously in case someone was in trouble. He rapped on the driver's window. He could see a dim figure at the wheel through the steamed-up glass. He opened the car door and Ruby's lifeless body and horribly contorted face slid out halfway, held by the seat belt.

Agatha Raisin was awakened the following morning by Toni with the news that Simon had been arrested for the murder of Ruby Carson. The CCTV cameras in the square had filmed her going to Simon's flat as had the one in the pedestrian area. But after the power cut, the cameras had stopped working.

Agatha swung into action, hiring a criminal lawyer, and then arrived at police headquarters to find that an exhausted Simon had just been released. The messages from Ruby, which he still had on his mobile phone, showed he had not wanted to see her. Chief

Superintendent Alistair White did not say he had been having an affair with Ruby but had said she had called him round to tell him of Agatha's find and that she was waiting for Simon.

He backed Simon's story that he had heard insulting remarks from Ruby about himself through the open window.

There was a tent over Ruby's car in the car park. Simon told Agatha the police reckoned that the murderer had been tailing Ruby and had smashed the back window and climbed into the passenger seat. A garrote had been found lying on the floor. It had been made from cheese wire with polished cylindrical pieces of wood attached.

"Surely there must be more than one person involved," exclaimed Agatha.

Despite the heat of the day, Simon shivered. He thought Ruby's dead contorted face would haunt him until the end of his days. "I feel some twisted mind is playing cat and mouse with us and knows our every move," he said.

Agatha stared at him. "Bugs!" she said. "I wonder if my cottage is bugged? We've got a radio frequency detector in the office. Go and get it, Simon, and I'll do a sweep of my home."

When they arrived, Charles was on the kitchen floor, playing with the cats. Agatha signalled him to be quiet and led him out into the garden where she told him about Ruby's murder and that they were going to sweep the cottage for bugs. "And what are my cats doing back here?" she asked.

"Doris is working upstairs," said Charles.

"What! This isn't cleaning day?"

"She thought the moggies might like to see their home again. I asked her to change the sheets in the spare room. I'd better get her and we can ask her if anyone could have got into the house while you were away."

Charles came back after a few minutes and led Doris to the bottom of the garden where Simon and Agatha were waiting. Asked if anyone could possibly have got in to bug the house, Doris wrinkled her brow, and then said, "There was only the telephone man. Some time ago it was. He said there was a fault on some of the village phones and they were checking them all. Oh, dear, I went upstairs and left him to it. Big heavyset man with a grey beard and glasses. One of them foreign accents. Could ha' been Polish."

"Anyone else?"

"Don't call anyone to mind. I'm right sorry, Agatha. Didn't cross my mind there would be anything up with him."

Agatha turned to Simon. "You'd better start sweeping for bugs. Start with the garden table and chairs."

They waited anxiously. Having finished with the garden furniture, Simon moved into the house. "Does he know what he's doing?" asked Charles.

"Yes, I get him to sweep the office from time to time," said Agatha.

"What puzzles me," said Charles, "is why you haven't been bumped off."

"You've forgotten. I was sent a poisonous bouquet."

"Maybe our murderer was sure you would recognise wolfsbane. If this place is bugged, then he would know you knew what the plant looked like. I think some psycho is playing with you, Agatha."

"That pseudo telephone man," said Agatha. "It sounds like someone in disguise. What about Tris Davent? He's got technical knowledge."

"You'd better tell the police about this, Aggie."

"What! And have to sit in that ghastly interview room again?"

"Just phone Bill. The police may have more sophisticated equipment. Still, with any luck, Simon won't find anything."

The sky above was turning darker. "I hope he finishes before it rains," said Doris.

"I'll phone Bill if Simon finds anything," said Agatha. "And how many times have I got to tell you not to call me Aggie! Jill's brother is pretty stocky. Add a false grey beard and glasses and he could be our bugger. An East European accent is easy to fake."

"'Bugger' being a good word to describe the horrible man, whoever he is," said Charles.

A warm drop of rain fell on Agatha's nose. "This is all we need," she said. "Let's get into the house and not say a word."

But when they entered, Simon was arranging four tiny bugs on the kitchen table. "All done, I hope," he said. "One in the phone, one under the computer desk, one behind the bookshelves and one behind your headboard upstairs, Agatha."

"I'll make us all a nice cup of tea," said Doris.

"Forget it. I'd like a gin and tonic," said Agatha. "Get it for me, Charles, and I'll phone Bill. He slipped me his mobile number so I won't need to be trapped by Wilkes."

Bill said to wait and he would be right over to make another sweep of the cottage.

Charles returned with Agatha's gin and tonic. She raised her hand to take the glass and Charles noticed that her hand shook. He put the glass down on the table and said gently, "Not getting the shakes, are you? Maybe not a good idea to start on the booze."

"It's not that," said Agatha. "This whole case is creeping me out. Some madman is out there, laughing at me, treating me like an amateur fool. But you're right, Charles. I am not going to start hitting the bottle. Pour it down the sink and make me a coffee instead. Are you all right, Simon?"

"That's why Ruby was murdered," he said wretchedly. "Someone listened in to everything I told you about her."

"My copies of that ledger!" Agatha jumped to her feet and raced through to her desk and rummaged frantically around. She came back and announced, "It's gone."

"So," said Charles, "the murderer must have got back inside somehow. Let's ask Doris." Doris had gone back upstairs. "I'll get her."

When Doris returned, Agatha asked, "Where do you leave the keys to this cottage?"

"At the foot of the stairs in my handbag," said Doris. "Oh, Agatha, dear. I've got a slip of paper in there with the burglar alarm code."

"So the bastard has been walking in and out when he felt like it," said Charles. "He is playing with you because he could have let himself in at night and murdered you."

Agatha phoned the security firm which had installed the burglar alarm and left a message to come as soon as possible and change the code. She then phoned a locksmith and asked him to change the locks.

The police arrived, headed by Bill and Alice, who introduced two technicians.

While the men got to work, they all moved back out to the garden, sheltering under the garden umbrella. Agatha told Bill about how the murderer had gained access to her cottage.

"You should find yourself another cleaner," said Alice.

"Never!" cried Agatha. "It was an easy mistake. No one is more honest or hardworking than Doris."

The only thing Asian about Bill were his beautiful almond-shaped eyes, now crinkled up in distress. "Agatha," he said. "Go away somewhere until all this is over. It's not safe here for you."

"What would be the point of that?" said Agatha. "You may never find this murderer who is turning out to be the serial killer of the Cotswolds. I can't leave my staff. They're in danger, too."

Agatha's phone rang. It was Phil Marshall. "I just dropped in to the office to get another camera and there is a young man here anxious to retain your services. He says he is Justin Nichols and Ruby was his stepmother during a previous marriage."

"I'd like to see him," said Agatha, "but I can't leave here just now." She told Phil what they had discovered and then said, "Give him directions and tell him to get over here."

When she rang off, she told Bill about Justin and then turned to Simon. "Did she say anything about being married before?"

"She said she was divorced," said Simon. "But there may have been another marriage before the last one. I think she kept her married name, Carson, which follows that before that marriage she could have been married to someone called Nichols."

The technicians came out to the garden to say they had finished their work and it seemed as if Simon had found all the bugs. Bill turned to Simon. "I hope you wore gloves."

"Yes," said Simon. "But if you plan on fingerprinting them, I bet our murderer wore gloves as well."

"We might be able to trace where they were bought. If you don't mind, Agatha, we'll stay on until this young man arrives. I'd like to hear what he has to say about Ruby."

Mrs. Bloxby arrived after the technicians had gone, saying she had been worried about village reports of police cars outside Agatha's cottage. Agatha told her everything that had happened. Her gentle face creased with worry. "It's as if someone is playing cat and mouse with you, Mrs. Raisin. But it does eliminate some suspects."

"Like who?" asked Agatha. "I don't see Gwen Simple being able to do anything so sophisticated as planting bugs," said the vicar's wife. "Miss Bannister is dead. Mrs. Simpson was never a suspect. Mrs. Tweedy is too old and would not have the energy or the technical know-how."

"My money is still on Gwen Simple," said Agatha. "She could have hired someone. I cannot believe for a moment she did not know what her murdering son was up to."

"We've had a watch on Gwen Simple for some time," said Bill. "She's had no strange callers, only people from the village of Ancombe. She helps out in the church and does a lot of good works."

"Humph!" snorted Agatha. "Could well be a smoke-screen."

"You're forgetting her ex," said Charles. "Davent runs a computer shop."

"How are you getting on with that ledger of accounts?" asked Agatha. She did not want to say her copy was missing, knowing that the police would not appreciate her actions.

"Don't seem to lead anywhere," said Bill. "But an awful lot of the entries are old. The ink's faded. There are very few new ones."

"Any news from America? I'll bet Jill was blackmailing one of her clients."

"It's been a laborious task checking everyone from America, particularly those with addresses in Chicago and the photos and stuff you found, but so far, nothing sinister. Not one of the men the Chicago police contacted would claim they were being blackmailed and there are ones with the wallets said they had had their pocket picked in some bar, anywhere but at the hotel. They're all married, you see."

Agatha clutched her shiny hair. "It could be anyone and we don't have a clue," she wailed. "I'm going to freshen up."

"I'm losing it," said Agatha to her bathroom mirror. "It's never affected me like this before. Get a grip!"

The day was humid and close. She showered and changed into a cool linen sheath and sandals and repaired her make-up.

The doorbell rang as she was descending the stairs. "I'll get it," she called.

"No you won't," said Bill, rushing to her side. "You don't know who is out there." Agatha stood back while he opened the door. She blinked. A young Adonis stood there with the watery sunlight gilding his blond hair. "I'm Justin Nichols," he said.

"Come in," said Bill. "This is Agatha Raisin. I am Detective Sergeant Bill Wong."

"Where's Phil Marshall?" asked Agatha.

"He dropped me off and went back to the office," said Justin.

Justin followed them into the kitchen, where the others were sitting around the table. Agatha made the introductions, urged him to sit down, took a chair herself and stared at him. His hair was naturally wavy. His skin was white and his eyes, an intense blue with thick lashes. He was wearing an open-necked shirt as blue as his eyes. He was slim but athletic-looking.

"How old are you?" asked Agatha.

"Twenty-five."

"But Ruby Carson was in her early forties. Was your father much older than Ruby when he married her?"

"Yes, he was fifty-five. I'm his only child. Mother had only been dead—she died of cancer—for two years when he met Ruby. She was only nineteen then. He was so much in love with her. But she up and divorced him two years later. He was devastated. He still obsesses about her and has commissioned me to employ you, Mrs. Raisin."

"What do you do, Mr. Nichols?" asked Alice Peterson.

"I'm a computer programmer. I'm freelance and I am taking a break between contracts. Why are you all staring at me like that?"

"Someone bugged my cottage," said Agatha, ignoring a warning signal from Bill. "Would you have the know-how?"

"No," he said innocently, "but I'm sure if I studied how to do it, I could manage, but why would I?"

"Did you like Mrs. Carson?" asked Bill.

"I thought she was a selfish, ambitious woman," he said. "But I'd do anything for my father. I resisted at first, asking why I should employ some village detective woman, but he persisted. Mind you, I did not expect to find you so attractive, Mrs. Raisin."

"Please call me Agatha." Her eyes were shining.

Surely not, thought Charles. He's much too young. Maybe it's just Agatha's maternal instinct.

"When was the divorce?" asked Bill.

"Years ago. Ruby was in sales and marketing and she suddenly announced she was going to join the police force. That was when she became insanely ambitious. All she would talk about was how she was going to be police commissioner one day. Dad hardly ever saw her. But the divorce hit him hard."

"What does your father do?"

"He's the managing director of Superfoods. That's how he met Ruby. She was doing the marketing for them."

Agatha suddenly wished they would all leave. "If you

follow me into the office," she said, "I'll draw up the contracts."

"Your secretary has already done that," said Justin.

"Look here," said Bill severely. "You are putting yourself in danger, young man. It is not only Mrs. Carson who has been murdered but other people as well! Whoever the murderer is, he seems to delight in getting rid of anyone who might help find out who he is. I strongly advise you to tear up the contracts and tell your father it is much too dangerous."

"I don't see why," said Justin. "I mean, I gather you've removed the bugs so no one will know Agatha is detecting on my behalf."

"Well, I've warned you," said Bill. "We'll be in touch, Agatha."

"I'd better go, too," said Mrs. Bloxby. "My husband will be wondering what has happened to me."

Agatha looked hopefully at Charles. "I'd better be off as well," he said. He had planned to stay, but, after all, the beautiful young man would certainly not be romantically interested in Agatha, and his presence might take Agatha's mind off her fears.

"Simon," said Agatha, "you'd better get on with that missing teenager case."

After Charles and Simon had gone, Agatha said reluctantly, "Leave it with me, Justin. Let me have your phone numbers and address. I'd better talk to your father as well."

She had planned to invite him to lunch but remembered in time that she had to wait at home for the locksmith and to have the code on the burglar alarm changed.

"It's lovely here," said Justin with a smile. "I've always wanted to see the inside of one of these old thatched cottages. Look, the rain has stopped."

"I'll be going now," called Doris from the hall.

Agatha rose to her feet and went to say goodbye.

When she returned, the kitchen was empty. She found Justin sitting at the table in the garden with the cats on his lap. "It's so quiet here," he said.

"I'm hungry," said Agatha. "Would you like to stay for lunch?"

"That would be lovely."

"Italian food okay?"

"Marvellous."

Agatha went in and phoned a local Italian restaurant that did deliveries and ordered two portions of escalope Milanese with salads and a bottle of Valpolicella.

She was just about to join him in the garden when the doorbell rang. Agatha peered through the peephole and saw Toni's pretty face looking back at her.

No, she thought. One look at Toni and he'll forget I even exist. She returned to the garden.

Agatha had never been attracted to younger men before. She guiltily remembered having a crush on that beautiful schoolteacher in Winter Parva, the one murdered by Gwen's son. Before she had always considered women who fell for men, just because of their looks, slightly . . . well . . . common. Yes, James was handsome but the same age as she was herself. Maybe Justin was gay. That was the trouble with beautiful men, they usually were.

A shadow fell across her. She swung round. Justin was looking at her quizzically. "Who was at the door?"

"I didn't open it," said Agatha. "Some salesman. I've ordered lunch. Should be here soon. Let's enjoy the garden."

Toni phoned Simon on his mobile. "Agatha's not answering the door. Is she all right?"

"That beautiful young man I phoned you about. I think our Agatha's smitten, so she won't want you around."

"That's ridiculous," said Toni.

"That's our Agatha," said Simon.

As Agatha talked about her previous cases, she decided that the attraction she felt for Justin was maternal.

Sometimes, infrequently, she thought it would have been nice to have children. She had felt strong maternal feelings for Toni, but that had unfortunately left her trying to manipulate the girl's life until she had backed off. So feeling much more comfortable, she chatted until the food arrived and they moved back into the kitchen.

Halfway through the meal, she remembered she was supposed to be detecting and asked Justin if his father had ever been in Chicago.

"I don't know if he's been in Chicago," said Justin. "I know he went to a couple of conferences in America, but that was when Mother was still alive."

"I think I had better meet your father," said Agatha. "Would this evening be convenient?"

"I should think so. I'll phone him when we've finished eating and set something up."

When Justin left, he kissed Agatha on the cheek. He had phoned his father and he would expect them at six o'clock. Justin said he would collect Agatha from her office.

After he had left, Agatha's hand involuntarily fluttered up to the cheek he had kissed. She felt suddenly lonely and old.

Reminding herself fiercely that any feelings she had for Justin were maternal, she forced herself not to change into something more glamorous. She called on Doris and gave her a new set of keys and the new code supplied by the locksmith, and set out for the office.

It was only when she arrived at the office that she realised the murderer could be someone in the crowds outside, watching to see who came and went. She phoned Justin and explained it would be safer if he just gave her directions to his home. Then she sadly opened a cupboard and took out a large box of disguises.

The frumpier the better, she thought. I must look like a worried client.

Before she changed, she took the precaution of phoning a car rental company and asked them to leave the car in the square and bring the keys and contract up to the office.

After she had paid for the car rental, she changed into a drab dress and flat shoes. On her head she put a plain dark wig that looked as if it had been badly permed. She stuffed pads in her cheeks and put on a pair of glasses. Leaning heavily on a stick, she eventually left the office, watched by a worried Mrs. Freedman.

The car was a new anonymous-looking black Ford. After studying the directions, she set off, with many nervous looks in the rearview mirror in case she was being followed.

The Nichols' house turned out to be a large mansion

on the edge of the town. A short gravelled drive led up to the house. Before she got out of the car, Agatha took the pads out of her cheeks and removed the glasses and wig. She carefully applied make-up and brushed her hair until it shone. She wriggled out of the dowdy frock, and was leaning over into the backseat to pick up her linen dress wearing only a brief lacy bra and knickers when a knock at the window made her jump. Justin was smiling in at her. Agatha lowered the window and said, "Get off with you and give me a moment. I'm just getting out of this disguise."

Justin grinned. "I was just admiring the view."

Cursing, Agatha slipped on her linen dress and a pair of high-heeled sandals, sprayed herself with La Vie Est Belle and walked up to the front door where Justin was waiting.

He kissed her warmly on the cheek. "You smell nice. Do come in. We're in the garden."

Although Agatha guessed the house had been built at the beginning of the twentieth century, the entrance hall looked dark and baronial. There were two suits of armour and beside them, two antique-looking carved chests. The floor was highly polished parquet with fine Oriental rugs placed like coloured islands across its expanse. Justin turned left and led her through a large drawing room. It somehow looked soulless, as if it had been put in the hands of an unimaginative interior designer. The carpet was mushroom-coloured, as was the velvet three-piece suite. An enormous flat screen TV dominated one wall. The coffee table had a glass showcase top holding a collection of medals. There were vases of silk flowers everywhere. French windows were open to the garden where a thickset grey-haired man sat at a table.

The air outside was heavy with the smell of roses. It was a magnificent garden with a smooth green lawn bordered by roses of every colour.

Mr. Nichols rose to meet her. He had once been a handsome man, Agatha guessed, but he now had one of those boozer's faces which looked as if the features had been blurred. His nose was thick and open-pored, his eyes a faded blue crisscrossed with red veins. He had a large drink on the table in front of him which smelled of vodka. Poor Justin, thought Agatha. Alcoholics will drink vodka, believing it has no smell.

Mr. Nichols had a potbelly, straining at the belt of his trousers.

He stood up and shook Agatha's hand. "Can Justin get you a drink?"

"It's all right. I'm driving," said Agatha. "But I wouldn't mind a black coffee."

"Justin," he ordered, "tell Mrs. Frint to make a pot of coffee and bring some biscuits as well. Now, I must find out who murdered poor Ruby. I still think about her a lot. I mean, I always hoped she would come back to me."

"You mean even after she walked out on you, you still have strong feelings for her?"

"I love her," he said.

"First I must warn you, Mr. Nichols, that there is a dangerous murderer out there. By employing me, you may put yourself in danger. This killer managed to get into my cottage and bug it. Is Mrs. Frint your housekeeper?"

"Yes, excellent lady."

"Then she must be told not to let anyone in the house—telephone, water, gas, anything like that even though whoever may seem to be carrying the right identification."

The watery, red-veined eyes of the perpetual drinker looked at Agatha with all the pleading of a beaten dog. "Find who killed my Ruby," he said.

Justin escorted Agatha out. He paused on the doorstep. "What about meeting for dinner one night so you can let me know if you have found anything?"

Agatha looked into those blue eyes and felt herself weaken. "We'd better meet somewhere pretty out of the way," she said cautiously. "I don't want the murderer coming after you."

"What about tomorrow night? There's the Black Bear in Moreton. Safe. Lots of people around. I could meet you there at eight o'clock."

Agatha's longing to have dinner with Justin fought with a dark image of murdered Herythe. Her longing won.

"All right," she said cautiously. "I'll make sure I'm not followed."

Chapter Eight

Agatha left the office early the following day, planning to spend time getting ready for the dinner with Justin. Of course, he was too young to fancy her, and surely she was too old to develop feelings for such a young man.

And yet, when she let herself into her cottage and found Charles in the kitchen, she was furious. "How did you get in?" she raged.

"Doris lent me her keys. She's worried about you being alone and so am I."

"Well, that's good of you," said Agatha, mollified.

"But I'm going out this evening and I don't want you around when I get back."

"Who are you meeting?"

"None of your business. Push off, Charles."

"He's too young for you."

"I don't know what you are talking about." Agatha made for the stairs. "I am going to change and I don't want you here when I get back."

But her plan for a leisurely hour and a half had been ruined. All the while she listened but could not hear any sign of him leaving. When she eventually went downstairs, it was to find the cottage empty and Doris's keys lying on the kitchen table.

Agatha fretted. Charles was really a good friend and had saved her so many times from sticky situations. Well, she would get him a set of keys, but after she saw how things progressed with Justin.

The evening was calm and serene, with a huge yellow moon floating above the village rooftops. Agatha remembered that blue moon. How odd it had looked. Although Moreton was only fifteen minutes away, she took a circuitous route down the backroads, past the Batsford estates office, checking all the time in the rearview mirror, but there was no one else on the road.

She hesitated outside the Black Bear. She was being

silly and all because this young man was beautiful. And by being silly, she could be putting him in danger.

"Are you going in or what?" demanded a man's voice behind her. "You're blocking the entrance."

"Sorry," mumbled Agatha. She pushed open the door of the dining room and went in.

Justin was seated at a corner table. He rose to meet her. "You look pretty," he said, kissing her on both cheeks.

No one had ever called Agatha Raisin pretty before. She gave him a radiant smile as she sat down opposite him.

Agatha had forgotten what huge servings they gave at this restaurant. She had ordered steak and ale pie and it made her waistline tighten just looking at it. Unfortunately, Justin said, "I cannot bear women who just pick at their food," so Agatha did her best and was relieved when Justin rose and said he needed to go to the loo. For one mad moment, she thought of tipping the whole thing into her handbag, but instead, she took it up to the counter and told the waitress to take her half-finished plate away.

"Good heavens!" said Justin when he returned. "I'll need to eat fast to catch up with you." He wanted to hear more about Agatha's adventures and so Agatha bragged happily, until Justin finished his meal and the waitress came up with the dessert menu.

"Nothing for me," said Agatha.

"I'm sure your son could manage something," said the waitress and Agatha could feel all her silly dreams crashing about her ears, even when Justin said gallantly, "Not my mother, my date."

Agatha suddenly could not wait for the evening to end. She thanked Justin for the meal and said she would be in touch with him as soon as she learned anything new.

Once home, she petted her cats, wondering whether to send them back to Doris for safety. But they were company and she felt lonely.

In the following weeks, Agatha and her detectives went about their work nervously, each one worried that they might be the murderer's next target, but nothing happened. Patrick reported that the police did not seem to have found anything new. Justin phoned a couple of times, inviting Agatha out, but each time she said it was not safe.

The agency seemed to be drawing in a lot of work: missing teenagers, divorces, firms who thought a member of the staff was stealing, a supermarket that claimed that liquor was disappearing, and so the list went on.

And while she worked, Agatha found her thoughts kept turning to Gwen Simple. She could not imagine Gwen having the strength to strangle anyone or to throw a body in the river, but she knew that men went weak at the knees in her company and wondered if she had an accomplice.

Mrs. Bloxby told Agatha that Gwen had started a business making silk flowers and would be selling them at a stall at Ancombe crafts fair at the week-end.

The vicar's wife said she would accompany her and they set off in Agatha's car.

"Have you see anything of Sir Charles?" asked Mrs. Bloxby.

"No, he disappears from time to time," said Agatha bitterly. "I sometimes think I could be lying dead on my kitchen floor for all he cares, and that goes for James, too. He went off on his travels and didn't even call to say goodbye. Here we are in Ancombe. Don't like the place."

"It's all right," said Mrs. Bloxby. "You've just had bad luck with some of the residents in the past. Look, you can park in that field next to the fair."

"They must think everyone drives a four-by-four," grumbled Agatha as her car bumped over the ruts in the field. She was directed by a Boy Scout to a remaining place at the far corner. "I didn't think it would be this busy," said Agatha.

"People come from all over," said Mrs. Bloxby. "They start stocking up for Christmas because you can get a lot of things here you can't buy anywhere else and the prices are reasonable."

As they wandered amongst the stalls, Agatha could not see the attraction. Did people actually give wooden salad bowls for Christmas? And if you wanted a concrete frog for your garden, how did you get it home?

"I'll find Mrs. Simple first," said Mrs. Bloxby, "and come back and let you know if she's with some man. I'll meet you in the refreshment tent."

Agatha bought a cup of tea and looked around for a place to sit down. All the tables were full. There was an elderly gentleman on his own so she went up and asked, "Is it all right if I sit here?"

"Go ahead." He squinted up at her through thick glasses. "But it ain't no use chatting me up. I'm spoken for."

"Never crossed my mind," said Agatha.

"Why?"

Agatha sighed. "You're too old for me."

"You ain't hardly a spring chicken yourself."

Agatha looked at his ancient face. "Do you mean women still chase you?"

"Like flies round a honey pot. All widders. Few of us men left down at the social club. Was married the once. Ain't what it's cracked up to be. Marriage, that's wot. Nag, nag, nag, from morning till night. When my Tilly was in her coffin I could swear I could hear her, going on and on and on."

Mrs. Bloxby came up to the table and Agatha said quickly, "Let's go outside."

Once outside the tent, she asked eagerly, "Anything?"

"She's got a very beautiful young man helping her. I'm afraid it's young Mr. Nichols."

"Surely not. It can't be!" exclaimed Agatha.

"I wish it weren't."

"I'd better have a look to make sure. No. Wait a moment. I've got his mobile number."

Agatha dialled. With a sinking heart, she recognised Justin's voice. "Don't say my name," she said. "I'm outside the tea tent."

She rang off and waited anxiously, jumping nervously when Justin came up behind her and said breezily, "Hullo, Agatha. I remember you. It's Mrs. Bloxby, isn't it?" Agatha said, "What are you doing helping Gwen Simple?"

"I'm detecting," said Justin. "Thought I'd lend a hand."

"Listen! She could be a murderess. It's not safe."

"I think she's all right. Mrs. Simple is very quiet and kind."

"She's as quiet and kind as a cobra," hissed Agatha.

"I said I would help her, so I am going back there," said Justin stubbornly. "I'll phone you later." And with that, he darted away through the crowd.

Despite the heat of the day, Agatha shivered. She had a sudden feeling of menace. But the crowds drifted back and forward, the village band played, the air was full of the smells of tea and cakes and it looked a safe, rural setting.

Later, while she waited for Justin to phone, Agatha worked through her notes. What if, she wondered, the murder of Ruby Carson had nothing to do with the other murders? And yet it had happened right after Simon had told her on the phone about Jill's book being found. She sighed. Simon could hardly go detecting in Oxford where police and detectives would be working hard to find out who had murdered Ruby.

When the doorbell rang, she went to answer its summons, expecting to see Justin but it was only Charles.

"Oh, it's you," she said. "I was waiting for Justin Nichols."

"The beautiful boy."

"I'm worried about him. He's decided to be a detective and to that end was helping Gwen sell silk flowers at the Ancombe fair."

"She's probably wrapped her coils around him."

"I tried to warn him," fretted Agatha. "Look, Charles, what do you think of this idea? What if the murder of Ruby has nothing to do with the others?"

Charles sat down at the kitchen table. The cats jumped onto his lap. "Now why do you think that?" he asked.

"Often people who are murdered are what Scotland Yard calls murderees. They set up dangerous scenarios which lead to them being killed. Ruby was having an affair with the police chief superintendent. He says he was just on a visit, but Ruby screamed of ambition and as we know from Simon, she coldly used sex as a weapon. Is the superintendent married? What if his wife knew of the affair? What do we know of the latest ex-husband? Perhaps she slept with other men to further her career and then dropped them. There is no record of her having contacted Jill Davent. It seems to me that our murderer wants to eliminate anyone who was close enough to Jill to reveal his identity."

Charles looked at her curiously. He knew, from past experience, that Agatha's seeming flights of fancy were based on sharp intuition.

"So we should start at the beginning," he said. "Let's go now and see Mr. Nichols and find out who she might have been having an affair with when she was married to him."

"I'll phone Patrick first and find out what he knows," said Agatha.

Patrick said that Ruby's last husband was a detective inspector called Jimmy Carson. He had an impeccable reputation. In fact, Patrick had been to see him. He had said that Ruby was difficult and was always throwing scenes. He had been glad to agree to an amicable divorce. He only saw his children from time to time because he was always busy.

"I didn't get a report from you about this," said Agatha.

"I was going to get round to it," protested Patrick, "but with so many suspects, it didn't seem top of the list. Also, Gwen Simple's phone has been bugged by the police for ages. Nothing there. Doesn't even get a call from her son."

"There are still such things as mobiles."

"Got that covered as well. Nothing."

"Send me over what you've got," said Agatha. "All of it. Even the stuff you don't think is important."

When she rang off, she said crossly to Charles, "I think Patrick is beginning to behave like the Lone Ranger." She told him what Patrick had said.

Charles shrugged. "Patrick's ex-police so he probably still feels loyalty to the plod. But he should have told you about Gwen's phones being bugged. Let's see what Nichols has to say for himself."

Mr. Nichols had been drinking, but was still coherent. Asked about Ruby, he went off into a paean of praise.

Agatha interrupted brutally. "Was she having an affair with Carson while she was married to you?"

"I didn't want to believe it," he said mournfully. "I wouldn't believe it, but Justin, poor little lad as he was then, was miserable. I said I'd prove him wrong and hired a detective. I was devastated at what he found out. I said I would forgive her, but she said it would be better for everyone if I agreed to a divorce. She said if I did that, I could keep Justin. If I didn't, she swore she would get custody. Justin pleaded to stay with me. What could I do? So I agreed to the divorce."

"Wait a minute," said Agatha. "She was only his stepmother. No court would give her custody."

"She said she would reveal some family secrets I didn't want exposed."

"What secrets?"

"They're secrets and that's how they'll stay!"

"So why are you still in love with this terrible woman?" asked Charles.

"Oh, she was a goddess when we were married. You don't know her. Carson seduced her. He's a wicked man. I'll bet he killed her."

"Was Justin fond of his stepmother?" asked Agatha.

"That's the sad bit," said Mr. Nichols. "He never forgave her."

"So why did he encourage you to engage my services?" asked Agatha.

"He said it was odd that we weren't getting any information from the police. He said we should try to find out something ourselves. He said it would put my mind at rest. He's a good boy and he loves his dad." Mr. Nichols raised his glass and took a large swallow of whisky.

His eyes filled with tears. "I wish I could have my Ruby back again."

They took their leave. "I think you're barking up the wrong tree, Agatha," said Charles. "Look, Ruby was garroted right after that message from Simon. That drunk in there is so advanced in alcoholism that he lives in a world of fantasy."

"Maybe he could have thought that if he couldn't have her, he would make sure no one else could," said Agatha.

"Did you have anyone else checking up on him?"

"I asked Simon to look into it."

Agatha phoned Simon. "Nichols is ex–Special Forces," he said. "You know, SAS, and they keep quiet about details."

When Agatha told Charles, he said, "That paints a different picture. He'd certainly know how to bump her off. But he's probably been sunk in booze for so long, I can't see him moving away from the chair and whisky bottle. Justin didn't say anything, but I doubt if Mr. Nichols had that job of his for a while."

When they were back in Agatha's cottage, Charles helped himself to a drink and moved out into the garden, followed by the cats. Agatha sat down at her computer and began to read everything on the murders.

After an hour, the doorbell rang. "I'll get it," called Charles. "I ordered Chinese food."

Agatha realised she was very hungry and followed him through to the kitchen, where he was placing containers on the kitchen table. "Dig in," he said. "I feel like beer. Got any?"

"No, but there's a bottle of white wine in the fridge."

They ate companionably, until Agatha suddenly put down her chopsticks and stared at him.

"Let's think about Justin," she said.

"Why?"

"Even as a child, he complained constantly about her. He must have wanted to be rid of her. What if he hated her?"

"Now there's a flight of fancy," said Charles. "Okay. I'll go along with it. Why wait so long?"

"It's a great opportunity," said Agatha. "Murders all over the place, one of them in Oxford. She's one of the investigating officers. What better time to bump her off? No one is going to look in his direction."

"But he hired you."

"What better way to find out what we know? What better way to feel manipulative power? I'll phone Simon and get him to dig up what he can on Justin."

"He'll have gone home."

"A bit of overtime never hurt anyone," said Agatha. She rang Simon. "You should ask Toni," he said.

"Are you being lazy or what?" asked Agatha.

"It's just that he came up to the office and he and Toni started chatting. Then he asked her out to dinner and a movie and she said yes."

"What movie?"

"Rerun of *Gigi* at the Arts Cinema."

When Agatha rang off, she stared at Charles in consternation as she told him the news.

"You're getting carried away," said Charles. "He's young and beautiful and so is she."

"I don't like this," said Agatha. "I'm going to hunt them down."

When Agatha entered the cinema, the film was nearly over. She blundered down in the darkness, shining a pencil torch on the faces of the audience, deaf to complaints.

She located them, sitting in the middle of a row halfway down. She found one empty seat behind them, feeling suddenly stupid. She was just thinking of getting up and leaving, when Toni turned round and saw her.

Toni experienced a flash of pure rage. Yes, Agatha had rescued her, not only from a drunken home, but from several other nasty situations. But that did not give her any reason to spy on her. She doesn't own me, thought Toni. She's always trying to control my life. The fact that Agatha had stopped doing just that escaped her mind. Young Toni often felt the weight of all that she owed Agatha a bit too heavily. It's better to give than receive—oh, thanks a bunch, Francis of Assisi—but say a prayer for the receivers, she mused.

Then common sense took over. If her date with Justin was important enough for Agatha to stalk her, always supposing Agatha was not jealous, and was not in the grip of one of her obsessions, then it followed that Agatha knew something sinister about her date.

When the film ended and the lights went up in the cinema, there was no sign of Agatha. Toni had suggested eating before the film, so, outside the cinema, she shook Justin's hand, said she would be in touch with him, refused his offer of a drink and made her way back to her flat. Upstairs, she looked out of her window and saw Agatha on the opposite side of the street, just turning away. Toni ran down and called out, "Agatha!"

Looking guilty, Agatha turned round. "Why were you stalking me?" asked Toni.

"Let's up to your flat and I'll tell you," said Agatha.

As she talked, Agatha began to feel her intuition had played her false. She had absolutely no proof of anything.

Toni listened carefully and then said, "You've had mad ideas before and they turned out to be right. Why don't we go with it? I know where Justin went to school. I'll see if I can find some of his old school friends. Say he hated Ruby, then he might have sounded off about it."

"Maybe I should do that," said Agatha. "I don't want to put you at risk."

"Don't mother me!" said Toni sharply. Then in a softer voice, she said, "I owe you a lot, Agatha, and sometimes I almost dislike you for it. Can you understand that?"

"I'll try," said Agatha, although she thought of how she had battled her way to success without help from anyone.

"Don't worry. I'll be careful," said Toni. "How old is he?"

"Twenty-six."

———

After Agatha had gone, Toni replayed in her mind the conversation she had had with Justin. Finally she remembered he had said he had gone to St. Jerome's School, a private school in Mircester. But he had not mentioned any school friends. Then she remembered that Simon had gone to the same school and phoned him up. After she had explained the whole thing, Simon said, "Maybe the local newspaper would have something. It's a prep school and they always covered prize givings. How old is he?"

"Twenty-five."

"So go to the local rag and look up prize givings for thirteen years ago. They all graduate when they're twelve."

Toni was a well-known figure at the *Mircester Chronicle*. She mounted the rickety wooden stairs to the editorial room and asked if she could look up the newspapers for twelve years ago. A secretary went away and reappeared with a large leather-bound book. "Not even on the old microfiche?" asked Toni.

"You know us," said the secretary. "We never move with the times, that's our motto."

Toni began to search, glad that it was a weekly newspaper. She concentrated on the July publications. She found the article and photographs of graduation day.

Justin had not received a prize. But there was a group photo. She only recognised him from his name amongst the others underneath the grainy photograph. He was wearing glasses. Those marvellous blue eyes, thought Toni. Must be contact lenses. She took notes of the names of three of the prizewinners, John Finlay, Henry Pilkington, and Paul Kumar.

Back in the office, she found a number for Henry Pilkington and called. A woman answered the phone. She said she was Henry's wife and that he worked as managing director of Comfy Baby on the industrial estate. She started to ask what it was all about but the wail of a child in the background distracted her and she hurriedly cut the call. Toni sent the information over to Agatha.

Agatha set out the following morning. Comfy Baby supplied goods for the new baby: cots, nappies, feeding bottles and clothes. The offices looked new and prosperous.

After waiting twenty minutes, she was ushered into the managing director's office. Henry Pilkington was a small man wearing thick rimless glasses. It was hard to believe he was the same age as Justin. He was bald on top and his thin brown hair was already going grey.

He studied Agatha's business card as if it were some

sort of poisonous insect. "So," he said, "she's done it at last."

Agatha looked bewildered. "Who's 'she'?"

"My bloody neurotic wife. Always accusing me of having an affair. How does she think I got this job so young? Leaving the office early? I've slaved and worked long hours to get where I am."

"I am not here because of your wife," said Agatha. "I would like to know about Justin Nichols."

His face cleared. "Oh, the golden boy. I was at prep school with him. Smarmy little creep. I'm telling you, the teachers fawned on him."

"Do you happen to know if his father's divorce hit him badly?"

"I wasn't one of his buddies. But I guess it did. I know he had long sessions with the school counsellor."

"Can you remember her name?"

"A Miss Currie."

"Do you know if she is still at the school?"

"No."

"Had Justin a particular friend?"

"I suppose John Finlay was close to him. He's working here. He's a sales rep. I'll see if he's around but he may be out on the road."

He picked up the phone and asked if John Finlay was in the building. Then Agatha heard him say, "Send him to my office."

169

Pilkington smiled at Agatha. "He'll be here in a few minutes. Good chap, but likes his drink."

When John Finlay arrived, Pilkington said, "You can use my office." He made the introductions and explained that Agatha wanted to know about Justin.

John Finlay was tall and handsome with thick curly black hair and an engaging smile. "I don't know if I can help you," he said. "I haven't seen Justin in ages. What's he done? Got a jealous wife?"

"Nothing like that," said Agatha, reflecting that the very name "private detective" immediately made most people think of divorce. "I'm interested in Justin's prep school days, particularly his reaction to his father's divorce."

"It hit him hard. He loathed his stepmother. Said she made his life hell, always sneering at him when she wasn't calling his father a waste of space. He was devoted to his father. He wanted to go on to Ratchett, the public school, but he did badly in the exams. His teachers intervened and managed to get him a place at Mircester High School, which is a state school. I remember now. There was a fire at the school in his final year and someone had seen him near the school on that night, but his girlfriend, Sadie Broody, stepped up and said he had been with her all night."

"Do you know where I can find Sarah Broody?"

"Haven't the faintest idea. What's this all about?"

"Nothing serious. Just checking up on something which hasn't got much to do with Justin. Thank you for your time."

When Agatha had left, Finlay was joined by Pilkington. They stood at the window and watched Agatha cross the car park and get into her car. "I like Justin," said John Finlay. "Might see if I can look him up and tell him that some detective has been asking questions about him. I mean, it was his stepmother who was murdered. Is that what she's investigating?"

Broody was not a common name and Agatha found an address for an S. Broody. Her flat was near Toni's. She rang the bell but there was no reply. By asking the neighbours, she learned that Sarah sold cosmetics at Jankers, Mircester's most expensive store.

Agatha was told that Sarah was on her lunch break and usually went to a café next door. The café was crowded. Agatha stared around at the customers. There was an attractive and elegant woman in the corner. Agatha approached her. "Miss Broody?"

The woman looked at her blankly. A woman at the next table swung round. "That's me. What do you want?"

There was an empty chair opposite her. Agatha slid into it. Sarah Broody was plain, there was no other word to describe her. She had large pale protruding eyes, bad skin and lank hair. Agatha wondered why, as she was a cosmetics saleswoman, she did not wear make-up.

Agatha explained who she was and then said she was interested in the night of the fire at the school. A red angry spot stood out on the sudden whiteness of Sarah's face. She began to gather up her things. "I have nothing to say."

"I only want to know why you lied," said Agatha, her bearlike eyes boring into Sarah's face. "It's either me or the police."

Sarah, who had half risen, sank back into her chair. "Bastard," she whispered. "Will I go to prison?"

"No, because I won't say a word," said Agatha. "It's all to do with another matter."

"He begged me. He said he would marry me if I lied for him. I would have done anything for him. I didn't sleep with him. He got hold of me the next day. I was dazzled. I said I would and I did. But the minute the schooldays were over, he dropped me. I was furious. I said I would tell the police the truth and he laughed and said I would go to prison for perverting the course of justice and he would even swear I had helped him. He's evil."

Agatha had a quick meal when she had left and went back to the office. Toni came in and asked her how she had got on and listened, alarmed. Then she said, "But why encourage his father to investigate? He was only a young boy when he was threatening her. I'm sure he's harmless."

"Look," said Agatha, "he tricked that poor girl into lying for him. He burned down the school. Murderers often start being arsonists when they are children."

"Do me a favour," said Toni. "If you are that sure he is evil, phone him up and say you have come to the conclusion that because of the huge investigation by the police in Oxford, it is hopeless trying to get anywhere. And after you have done that, phone the police and report your findings about the school fire."

But Agatha felt her report on the fire could wait. Right at that moment, she could not bear the idea of another interrogation at police headquarters.

However, she phoned Justin on his mobile and explained her reasons for dropping the case. To her relief, he took the news without protest, only saying, "I see what you mean. I'll tell Dad. He'll understand."

Agatha then turned her attention to another outstanding case and got to work. By the end of the day, she felt exhausted. The case meant she had to follow a nimble possible adulteress, on foot, accompanied by Phil with his cameras. The humid weather did not help. Nor did her high-heeled sandals. The woman in question went from shop to shop, then she dropped into a café for coffee before resuming her shopping and then blamelessly returned home to her suspicious husband, carrying bags of purchases while Agatha cursed a woman who wore trainers and never seemed to bother taking her car out.

She returned to her cottage, put a microwave meal in for dinner, fed her cats and finally settled down in front of the television, flicking through the channels to see if she could find a bit of escapism. She finally found an episode of *Morse* she had not seen before, but after the first half hour, her eyes drooped and she fell asleep.

Charles let himself in later that evening. He saw Agatha asleep on the sofa and decided to leave her and wake her later on. He went upstairs and put his bag in the spare room. He was just about to go downstairs when he heard the doorbell ring. He stood and listened. Then he heard Agatha making her way to the door, saying, "Justin! Can this wait? I'm very tired."

And then Justin's voice. "It'll only take a moment."

Charles wondered what to do. Agatha had seemed smitten by Justin, then suspicious of him. She might be furious to find him lurking around. He sat down at the top of the stairs and waited.

In the kitchen, Agatha went over to the coffee percolator and asked, "Coffee?"

"Not for me, thank you."

"I'll have one," said Agatha. "I'm barely awake." Her eyes fell on her open handbag, lying on the counter with the electric light gleaming on the edge of her tape recorder. She poured herself a cup of coffee, and, before turning around, switched on the tape recorder.

Justin was already sitting at the kitchen table. Agatha sat down opposite him.

"I had a call from the Broody female," he said. "Broody by name, broody by nature. She was sobbing and gulping and saying she had betrayed me but if I would only see her again, she would swear blind she had told you nothing. Then an old school friend phoned my dad and said you'd been asking odd questions of what I was like at the time of the divorce. May I remind you, sweetie, that you are being paid to investigate my stepmother's death?"

"I know that," said Agatha. "Look, I'm tired. Can't this wait until tomorrow?"

"No, it can't wait. You want the truth? Well, listen to this. Ruby made my life hell and she drove my father into alcoholism. I've dreamt for years of a way to get rid of her and you gave me that way. All those murders. Who would suspect me if another one was committed? So I watched and waited outside her house for an opportunity. That night I followed her to Mircester. I saw her park her car in the middle of that storm. I guessed the CCTV cameras wouldn't be able to pick up anything because of the power cut and there was another crack of thunder and I broke the glass of the back window of her car."

That beautiful face seemed to Agatha the epitome of evil. She had been trying to give up smoking but now she grabbed her packet of cigarettes and lit one up.

He grinned. "Last cigarette before the execution?"

Then he dodged as Agatha seized a milk bottle off the table and threw it at him. From his pocket, he produced a length of wire with a piece of wood at the end. Agatha jumped to her feet and made for the garden door. He seized her and bore her down onto the floor.

"Help me!" screamed Agatha as the cruel wire went round her neck.

Then suddenly he went limp. Panting, Agatha rolled out from under him and struggled to her feet. Charles was standing there with a poker in his hand.

"Got anything to tie him up?" he asked. "I hope I haven't killed him."

With shaking hands, Agatha jerked open a kitchen drawer and pulled out a roll of garden twine.

"Phone the police," ordered Charles. "I'll tie him up after I find out if he's still breathing."

While Agatha phoned, he tied Justin's hands and feet and then checked his pulse. "He's alive. Hope I haven't given the bastard brain damage or we won't get a confession."

"I got it on tape," said Agatha. Her face was chalk white and her legs seemed to have turned to jelly.

Justin recovered consciousness. "You've got nothing," he whispered. "I'll deny the whole thing."

Agatha fumbled in her handbag and took out the tape recorder. She ran the tape back and then pressed the button to play it. Appalled, Justin heard his voice coming over loud and clear.

Charles and Agatha were finally left alone, after a long night. Agatha wondered how Justin's father would survive the news. It transpired he had been sacked from his job months before for drunkenness. Agatha had not been thanked for her detective work and Charles had been grilled about whether he thought he had used reasonable force.

"Aren't you going to phone the press and tell them it was you who solved Ruby's murder?" asked Charles.

Agatha took a swig of black coffee and lit a cigarette. "I've been warned not to speak to the press. Everything is sub judice before the court case."

"I could leak it for you."

"Don't do that," said Agatha wearily. "Wilkes would come down on me like a ton of bricks."

"You're a very good detective, Agatha."

"I sometimes wonder."

"Who else would have sensed there was something up with Justin?"

Agatha scowled into her drink. She was suddenly sure that her suspicions about Justin had been prompted by jealousy when she had seen him with Gwen Simple.

She sighed. "Maybe the police would have got round to it anyway."

There was a ring at the doorbell. "Ignore that," said Charles.

"No, I'll go."

Agatha came back into the kitchen followed by Mrs. Bloxby and James Lacey.

"What's been happening?" asked James. "I've just got back and heard in the village shop about your cottage swarming with police."

"I was worried, too," said Mrs. Bloxby. "By the time the Chinese whispers reached the vicarage, I heard you had been arrested."

"I'll make a pot of coffee," said Charles, "and Agatha can tell you all about it."

"Get me another coffee," said Agatha. "I can hardly keep my eyes open."

As Agatha recounted her adventures, she began to feel the whole thing was unreal, that she had imagined it all. When she had finished, James said, "Now all you have to do is solve the other murders."

Charles entering with a tray of coffee said sharply, "I think Agatha should leave that to the police."

James laughed. "Oh, Agatha won't leave it alone. She's as tough as old boots."

"Look," said Charles, "she's just escaped being murdered. The best thing she can do is take a few days off and chill out."

Both men glared at each other.

I think they are both in love with her in their odd ways, thought Mrs. Bloxby. Oh, why doesn't Agatha get married and settle down?

James gave a reluctant laugh and turned to Mrs. Bloxby. "You must long for the days when there weren't so many incomers."

"Well, Mrs. Simple and her son had been in Winter Parva for some time. I wonder how many murders went unnoticed before all this expert technology." said the vicar's wife. "But do forget about these murders, Mrs. Raisin. Be safe."

"I'll think about it," said Agatha.

Chapter Nine

B ut that night, as she tossed and turned in bed, Agatha felt she simply could not let go. The murderer was out there, and, if not stopped, would kill again. The next target might be me, thought Agatha. She had kept her bedside light on to banish the fears brought by darkness. She regretted having bought a thatched cottage because nameless creatures rustled in the thatch.

Her bedroom door opened and Charles, who had been sleeping in the spare room, walked in, wrapped in a dressing gown.

He was carrying a glass of milk. "Drink this," he ordered. "And here's a sleeping pill. I picked up a prescription today for my aunt. She won't miss one."

"I don't drink milk and I never take sleeping pills," complained Agatha.

"Do as you're told for once in your life," said Charles, "or I will ram this pill down your throat."

"Oh, all right," said Agatha grumpily. She swallowed the pill. Then she said, "I never thanked you for saving my life."

"All in the day's work," said Charles. "Go to sleep."

After he had left, Agatha felt she would never sleep when she suddenly plunged down into a dream where Justin was chasing her round a village fair with an ax.

Agatha arose late next morning to find that Charles had left. Patrick Mulligan phoned her to tell her that Justin had taken poison on the road to the police station. He had died horribly. They thought it might be cyanide but were waiting for the results of the autopsy. The three officers who had been driving him to headquarters were in trouble because they had not handcuffed him. There was worse to come. The news was broken to Mr. Nichols, who had said he would identify the body. He had asked Bill Wong and Alice Peterson to wait while he changed. When they felt he was taking too long about it, they had gone up to his bedroom to find the door locked. Bill had finally managed to break it down to find that Justin's father had hanged himself.

"Where on earth does one get a cyanide pill in this day and age?" asked Agatha. "And why didn't they tell Charles that Justin had committed suicide instead of leaving him to worry that he might have caused brain damage?"

"Search me," said Patrick. "In fact, the officers are also being berated for not having searched him before they put him in the car."

When he had rung off, Agatha took a cup of black coffee into the garden and sat down and watched her cats chasing cloud shadows across the grass. The air was full of the scent of flowers. The birds were quiet as they always were in August.

Agatha finished her coffee and decided to walk up to the vicarage. With all the murder and mayhem, she had forgotten it was Sunday. People were leaving the church, stopping to shake hands with the vicar. The women in bright dresses, the happy chatter, all looked so safe. Agatha was about to turn away when she heard her name being called and swung round. Mrs. Bloxby came hurrying to meet her.

"Come back to the vicarage," said the vicar's wife, "and we'll have a quiet drink and chat in the garden."

"Won't your husband mind?"

"Alf has got to rush off to Winter Parva to conduct another service."

They started to walk towards the vicarage when Agatha stopped abruptly.

"What's up?" asked Mrs. Bloxby anxiously.

"Nothing," said Agatha. "I'm still a bit nervous." But Agatha could have sworn that just for a moment she had sensed something evil, and then decided it must be the aftereffects of that sleeping pill.

Once in the vicarage garden, Agatha sat sipping sherry instead of her usual gin and tonic. Sherry seemed such a *holy* drink and surely the God that Agatha only believed existed in times of stress would approve and not send any more frights down into her life.

"What do you get out of believing in God?" she asked abruptly.

"Comfort," said Mrs. Bloxby.

Snakes and bastards, thought Agatha, I must be going soft in the head.

"Is Sir Charles not still with you?" asked Mrs. Bloxby.

"No, he melted away like the Cheshire cat as usual," said Agatha.

"And did James call this morning to see how you were?"

"Not him. He thinks I'm made of iron."

"How did Charles get into your cottage?"

"In a weak moment, I sent him a set of keys. Just as well, or I'd be dead by now."

"Have you ever considered," said the vicar's wife cautiously, "that Sir Charles's pretty constant presence is stopping you from finding a suitable man?"

Agatha sighed. "I wish I could say that were the case. But only unsuitable men come my way and he's often been there, to save me from them." She paused. "I wonder if I should search round the village for wolfsbane."

"The police did a thorough search for that plant, not only in this village but in all the villages round about," said Mrs. Bloxby. "Try to relax and leave it all to them."

But when Agatha left, she felt she would never rest until she found out the identity of the murderer.

Once more on her own, she realised she was hungry and headed for the Red Lion. The pub had become a gastro pub, which meant the same old food with the usual gastro pub descriptions. Salads were "drizzled" with vinaigrette. There was a soup of "foraged" greens. Cheese on toast was described as "whipped goat's curd, garden shoots and pickled alliums." She ordered the "taste of Italy, home-cooked lasagne with hard-cut chips." "What are hard-cut chips?" Agatha asked the landlord, John Fletcher.

"Because it's hard to get the frozen ones out of the bag," he said.

"And you don't even blush," said Agatha. "Okay, I'll have the lasagne and a glass of Merlot."

"You'll be sitting outside then," said John, "so you can smoke."

"I've given up," lied Agatha because she wanted to join the ranks of the saintly nonsmokers.

John gave her a cynical look. "Well, if you change your mind, let me know."

"Forget the chips," said Agatha. "I'll have the shaved salad instead. What's a shaved salad?"

"I prepared it while I was shaving," said John.

"Oh, ha, so very ha." Agatha retreated to a table. A television set was mounted over the bar with the sound turned down. Richard Dawkins, that celebrity agnostic, was mouthing away about something, no doubt trying to mess up someone's Sunday, thought Agatha. Funny how Christianity bashing had become so fashionable. She waved to various people she knew but no one came over to her table. Agatha realised that once again the village associated her with murder. Was her conviction that somehow Gwen Simple was behind it the wrong one?

Her food arrived. It looked like the same old pub grub they had served before the fancy menus. She ate mechanically, turning over what she knew about the murders in her mind.

Agatha still felt shaken after the latest attempt on her life and had a longing to finish her meal, go home, go to bed and pull the duvet over her head. But, instead, she decided to drive to Ancombe and spy on Gwen.

Gwen was hosting a small party in her front garden. She was wearing an old-fashioned sort of tea gown of some gauzy patterned material, which floated about her body. Her hair was piled on top of her head. Her long thin nose and hooded eyes in her white face made her look more than ever as if she had stepped down from some mediaeval painting. Agatha stood behind a tree at the corner of the garden to shield herself from the guests. Two late arrivals walked past her and made their way into the garden.

Agatha noticed that a very handsome man was helping serve the drinks. He was as tall as James but with red hair and a tanned face. The new arrivals said something to Gwen, who looked straight at the tree behind which Agatha was hiding. She said something to the handsome man, who strode down the garden. Agatha was scurrying off to her car when he caught up with her.

"Mrs. Simple wants to know what you are doing spying on her," he said.

"I am a private detective and—"

"So she told me. What are you doing here?"

"Mrs. Simple is one of the suspects in a detective case I am investigating."

"The fact that her wretched son is a murderer doesn't make her one. She is phoning headquarters to put in a claim of harassment."

"Snakes and bastards. They'll be down on me like a ton of bricks. When that chap nearly murdered me, they treated me as if I were a villain."

He looked curiously down at her. The sun was shining on Agatha's shiny hair. She was wearing a white shirt blouse with a short skirt, which showed off her excellent legs. A faint scent of Miss Dior drifted round her.

"I've just got back from Dubai. What's this about you nearly being murdered?"

"Don't you think you'd better introduce yourself?" said Agatha.

"I am Mark Dretter. I have just taken a cottage in Ancombe."

"Look," said Agatha, wishing she had worn low heels because the straps of her high-heeled sandals were beginning to become uncomfortable, "I'm tired of standing in the heat. Can we talk somewhere more comfortable?"

"Why not? I only met Gwen today when she called on me and invited me to her party. Where do you suggest?"

"I can drive you to the pub in Carsely and we can talk there."

"You lead the way," said Mark, "and I'll follow you."

How old is he? wondered Agatha. I think he's about my age. He's very good-looking and he's got a great physique. Could he have been lying? Maybe he's close to Gwen and wants to find out what I know. Oh, I do hope Charles doesn't choose to make one of his sudden appearances.

At the Red Lion, they chose a table in the garden. To her surprise, he ordered a bottle of cold white wine.

"Aren't you worried about being caught for drunk driving?" she asked. "It's all right for me. I can leave my car here and walk home."

"I'll be quite safe," said Mark. "It's only a few miles to Ancombe and I don't plan to get drunk."

"Before I tell you all about it," said Agatha cautiously, "when did you arrive back from Dubai?"

"Yesterday. I got my sister to choose a cottage in the Cotswolds for me and I wired her the money."

"And what do you do?"

"I work at the British embassy. I'm on leave."

"Spook?"

"Not me. Just an underling. Now let's hear about this murder."

"Murders," corrected Agatha.

He listened intently as Agatha told him the whole story, ending up with Justin's attempt on her life.

When she had finished, he said, "And I was hoping for a quiet life in an area where nothing bad happens. But it seems a bit hard to suspect Gwen just because of her awful son."

"How did you hear about that?" asked Agatha.

"My sister told me."

"But not about the other murders? You get the British newspapers in Dubai. You must have read something."

"It's all coming back to me. Yes, I did read about it. For a start, I wasn't aware Carsely was so close and the other murders took place in Oxford."

With one of her sudden flashes of intuition, Agatha thought, he's lying. Gwen's already snared him and he's doing his best to find out what he can and report back to her.

Agatha rated her own appearance very low. It never dawned on her that this was caused by her previous bad taste in men. Those experiences that had reduced her self-worth. Suddenly she realised he was speaking.

"It seems to have started with that therapist," he said. "The fact that when she was in Chicago, she was a hooker makes things difficult. Look at it the other way. People in this village went to Jill for counselling. Someone was afraid that Oxford detective had found out something. Then there is the barrister. Perhaps the murderer knew from your bugged cottage that he was going to be investigated and overrated his abilities. Now we come to Victoria Bannister. What was she like?"

"Bitch. Nosy. Jealous. Spinster."

"Right. She spied on you. She may have known who went to consult Jill. Just maybe she fancied herself as a sort of Poirot and went around accusing Jill's clients, saying, you are the murderer. If it hadn't been for the Chicago connection, you would have concentrated on this village. I mean, wolfsbane suggests someone with a good knowledge of plants."

Agatha was feeling more and more attracted to Mark. But there was one thing she had to get clear. She told him about the few in the village that she knew had gone to Jill. "Why did you lie to me when you said you knew nothing of the murders? Gwen got her hooks into you when she called to invite you to her party. She told you all about her son and how this private detective was persecuting her. You were even acting as host at her garden party. Like a knight errant you probably phoned her from your car on the road here and told her you were on the case."

He gave a reluctant laugh. "Now you've made me feel like a fool. Gwen told a pathetic story and I was sorry for her. I thought I was going to scare off some hard-faced bat instead of a woman with shiny hair and smelling of summer. Look here, let's forget about Gwen and be friends."

His hair was thick and red with threads of silver shining in the sun.

"Are you married?" asked Agatha.

"No. My poor wife died of cancer three years ago. And you?"

"Divorced. Any children?"

"No. And you?"

"None either."

He smiled at her across the table and Agatha's treacherous heart gave a lurch. "You didn't answer my question. Friends?" He held his hand across the table.

Agatha shook it. "Friends," she echoed.

"Why don't we have dinner tomorrow night?"

"Perhaps," said Agatha cautiously. "Give me your card and I'll phone you. I often have to work late."

"We haven't drunk much of this wine," said Mark. "I'd better get back to the party."

"And what will you report?"

"That a charming lady such as yourself can have no evil intentions. I'll phone you."

As soon as he had gone, Agatha lit up a cigarette. The bottle was almost half full but she did not feel like drinking any more. She could feel a rising bubble of excitement. Agatha often had dreams of being married. Would she need to remove to Dubai? But then reality took over. Men such as Mark did not want to marry middle-aged women. They usually wanted some young charmer of child-bearing age. She wondered what tales of persecution Gwen was regaling him with.

A shadow fell across the table. Agatha looked up. "Drinking alone?" asked James.

"No, I had company," said Agatha. "Get yourself a glass and you can have some of this wine before it gets too warm."

When James returned and poured himself a glass of wine, he asked, "Have you got over your fright of having been nearly killed?"

"Mostly. I feel I should maybe rent a flat in Mircester. My cottage just does not seem safe. But I don't like to think of my cats being stuck in a city flat."

"Then let Doris have them."

"Perhaps."

"Drink is not the solution. Unlike you to order a whole bottle."

"I didn't order it. As I said, I had company. He's just left."

"Who's 'he,' Agatha?"

Agatha proceeded to tell him the whole story, about

how she had been caught spying on Gwen and how she had become friends with Mark.

"Go carefully," counselled James when she had finished. "I've got contacts in Dubai. I'll check on him."

"He put an idea in my head," said Agatha. "If Gwen has nothing to do with it, then perhaps the Oxford murders and the sophistication of bugging my house has turned me away from the people in Carsely. You know how it is these days with Cotswold villages. There are London people who only use a cottage for week-ends. Any of them you know about?"

"I've talked to some of the wives who are left down in the village all week, waiting for their husbands to come home at week-ends. They have to find amusement to pass the time. Going to a therapist when you don't really need one is an ego trip. Just sit or lie there with a captive audience and talk about yourself."

"Any particular one you can think of?" asked Agatha.

"There's Bunty Rotherham. She's married to Oran Rotherham, who has an electronics factory in Slough."

"What sort of name is Oran?"

"It means pale green in Irish Gaelic."

"Whereabouts is his house?"

"It's just outside the village on the Ancombe road. You can't see it from the road. There is a disused gatehouse with bricked-up windows at the foot of the drive, about half a mile from Carsely."

"How do you know all this?"

"I was invited there to a party one week-end. They've got the lot: swimming pool, hot tub, tennis courts and croquet lawn."

"What sort of man is Oran?"

"Powerful and belligerent. Strong Irish accent except when he forgets to use it and bits of Cockney start creeping in. Suspected a few years ago of selling remote control devices to the Iranians, but the intelligence services couldn't find anything to charge him with."

"I'll go and call on him now," said Agatha.

"I'd better go with you," said James. "I gather you were rude to the trophy wives one evening."

"Well, let's hope Bunty wasn't one of them. I'll pay for this wine. Charles has me well trained."

But the landlord told her that Mark had paid for the wine. When she thought of him, a rosy, warm feeling enveloped her.

James suggested they take his car as Agatha confessed to having drunk two glasses of wine.

To Agatha's dismay, James had just bought a white Morgan sports car, difficult to get in and out of. James turned in past the deserted lodge and cruised up a long drive bordered on either side by tall pine trees. The house finally came into view. It was a large white fairly modern house which resembled a bathing lido. "Looks like something out of Poirot," said James. "I would guess it was built in the thirties by some architect trying to copy Lutyens. Funny, isn't it, that anything round here built in the thirties we think of as modern."

James parked the car beside a large Bentley and a Porsche. "At least they don't seem to have guests," he said.

Agatha tried to get out of the low-slung sports car and ended up landing on her bottom on the gravel.

"Bloody car," she grumbled as James helped her to her feet.

"There is nothing up with my car," said James. "If you would stop wearing tight skirts and those ridiculously high heels, you wouldn't have any trouble."

"That was what was up with our marriage," said Agatha furiously. "Always running me down and criticising my clothes."

"Oh, shut up," snapped James. "Do you want to visit this man or not?"

He marched towards the front door and rang the bell, not looking round to see if Agatha was following.

Agatha tottered after him, the thin heels of her sandals finding it difficult to cope with the gravel.

James turned round when she caught up with him. "Maybe there's nobody home."

A female voice suddenly sounded tinnily over the intercom beside the door. "Who is it?"

"James Lacey."

"Oh, darling James. Wait a moment."

The sun beat down. Looking up at the building, Agatha noticed that it consisted of a lot of curved balconies and many plate glass windows.

The door swung open and a butler stood there in a black suit, black tie and white shirt. He looked thuggish, what Agatha privately damned as a knuckle dragger. "They're at the pool," he said in a raspy voice. "Follow me."

They passed through a hall with white walls. A curving stone staircase, also white but with a black wrought iron banister, led upwards. Then into a large room where everything seemed white from the leather sofa and armchairs to the white walls on three sides, the fourth being large windows. A coffee table held copies of the latest glossy magazines. A white nude sculpture of a woman dominated the room. The windows were open onto a terrace. The man trotted in front of them. Agatha noticed that despite the formality of his dress, he was wearing trainers. Maybe he wasn't really a butler but some sort of strong-arm man. They walked down steps from the terrace to the back of the house where a man and a woman were sprawled in their swimming costumes on loungers beside a table. Bunty was wearing a skimpy bikini over her salon tan. Agatha realised thankfully that she was not one of the women she had insulted in the pub. Oran rose from his lounger and sat on the end of it. His chest was covered in a thick mat of black hair. He had a black beard and moustache. Even the backs of his powerful hands were hairy.

Bunty was the picture of a trophy wife from her pout mouth, collagen enhanced, to her painted toenails. "Roger," she said, "bring chairs and we'll all sit round the table and have drinkies."

Had Roger really muttered a four-letter word before he turned away? He certainly didn't seem to like taking orders from Bunty. But he came back in a few moments, pushing four fold-up chairs on a trolley. He opened them up and set them round the table. Bunty uncoiled from the lounger and sat at the table, waving a hand at Agatha and James, diamond rings flashing in the sun, to indicate they should do the same. Oran heaved his powerful bulk into another chair. "What'll yiz be havin' in the way o' a drink?"

"Nothing for me," said James. "I'm driving and I've already reached my limit."

"Not for me, either," said Agatha.

Bunty pouted and called to Roger, "Fix me a tequila." Roger scowled but disappeared inside the house.

"So what's the reason for the visit?" asked Oran.

"My cottage was recently bugged," said Agatha. "Do you or your wife know of anyone in the village with the knowledge to do it?"

His eyes were suddenly hard. "Apart from me, d'ye mean?"

"Of course," said James quickly.

"Not a clue," said Oran. "If that's all you came about, you'd better clear off. Roger!"

Roger promptly appeared. "See them out," said Oran. He returned to the lounger and closed his eyes.

"That man's a villain, if ever there was one," said Agatha, after she had shoe-horned herself into James's car.

"I think he's just a rather bluff self-made man," said James.

"No, he's a villain," protested Agatha, "and that Roger is enough to give anyone the creeps."

"Okay," said James, swinging the car out of the drive and onto the Carsely road, "let's say you're right. Can you imagine him consulting Jill?"

"No, but Bunty might," said Agatha. "She's stuck in the country all week. You have to be pretty narcissistic to get all the body work she's had done. Did you notice those breasts?"

"Couldn't take my eyes off them," said James, and Agatha glared at him.

"Silicone if I ever saw it," said Agatha. "And that wind-tunnel face-lift. So she trots along to Jill to talk about herself and maybe talks too much about the shifty side of Oran's business. He gets alarmed and bugs my cottage to find out what we know."

"Agatha, I went to one of their parties and it was full of the great and the good of the Cotswolds."

"And did anyone ask about me?"

"Several people. You are by way of being a village celebrity."

"Did Bunty or Oran ask about me?"

"Not that I can remember. Here we are. I am sure you are sober enough to drive home."

This time, James came round and hauled Agatha out of the passenger seat.

"I may see you tomorrow," he said, "but I've got a lot of writing to do."

Agatha remembered Mark Dretter's invitation to dinner. "Don't force yourself," she said. "I'm going to be too busy."

Instead of going home, Agatha drove to the vicarage, reflecting that living in the country made one lazy. In London, she had walked miles. In the country, she had developed the habit of driving even short distances.

The vicar answered the door and glared at her. He

turned and walked away but he left the door open. Agatha followed him in and heard his voice shouting, "That Raisin woman is here again. Why don't you just invite her to stay?"

Mrs. Bloxby appeared. "Oh, let's go into the garden. The day has turned quite humid and there's not a breath of fresh air. What can I get you?"

"Nothing," said Agatha. "I want to talk."

Agatha sank down into a garden chair and eased her tortured feet out of her sandals. "James and I went to see the Rotherhams. I think he's a thug."

"A very generous thug," said Mrs. Bloxby. "He gave five thousand pounds to the village sports club and two thousand to the church repair fund."

"I didn't even know that house of theirs existed," said Agatha.

"They bought it six months ago," said Mrs. Bloxby. "It was nearly a ruin and they must have spent a fortune repairing it."

"Do they have any servants apart from a thug called Roger?"

"They get the cleaning done by a firm in Evesham and engage a catering company if they are entertaining. He has the most peculiar stage Irish accent."

"I wonder if he ever went to Chicago," said Agatha.

Mrs. Bloxby leaned back in her chair and closed her eyes. She looked tired. Who would be a vicar's wife?

thought Agatha. Dogsbody, nurse, therapist, always kind, always tactful. No pay and very little thanks.

"Isn't it nearly your birthday?" she asked.

Mrs. Bloxby opened her eyes. "It's tomorrow."

"Going out to celebrate?"

"I shouldn't think so. Alf always forgets."

"I've got to go. Remembered something. Don't get up. I can see myself out."

Once back in her cottage, Agatha sat down at her computer and wrote out a flier and printed off a pile of copies. The flier said, "IT IS MRS. BLOXBY'S BIRTHDAY TOMORROW. SEND A CARD TO OUR HARDWORKING VICAR'S WIFE."

Putting on a pair of flat walking shoes, she set out round the village, shoving fliers through letter boxes until she felt too tired to go on.

Returning to her cottage, she remembered she had an unopened bottle of Chanel No. 5 that James had given her for Christmas last year. She found some fancy wrapping paper in a drawer in the kitchen and wrapped it up. Then back to the computer to send an e-mail gift card. She would leave the scent on the doorstep of the vicarage in the morning before she went to work. It was a Sunday and most of the shops now closed. She could only hope that some people in the village could manage to send birthday wishes.

Mrs. Bloxby was preparing her husband's breakfast the following morning when the doorbell rang. Before she could open the door, she had to clear away a great pile of mail. When she did open the door, a florist's van was parked outside. "You've got a lot of bouquets," said the deliveryman. "I'll carry them inside for you. You'd better move all these parcels off the doorstep so I don't trip."

Mrs. Bloxby stood amazed as he carried bouquet after bouquet into the vicarage.

The vicar appeared. "What's going on here?" he demanded.

"It's my birthday," said his wife. "Look at all the flowers! And can you help me get all those parcels that are on the doorstep? I'll take most of the flowers to decorate the church. How lovely. Interflora must have been working overtime."

The vicar stood staring at his wife like a deer caught in the headlamps. Then he said, "Back in a minute."

He rushed to his study. He had recently been at an auction with a friend and on impulse had bid for a pretty gold Edwardian brooch inlaid with moonstones and small chip diamonds. He had planned to give it to his wife on their wedding anniversary in November. It came in a red morocco leather box. He took it out of the locked drawer at the bottom of his desk and hurried back with it. His wife was reading the cards on the flowers. "Here," he said gruffly. "Happy birthday."

"Oh, Alf," said Mrs. Bloxby, opening the box. "It's beautiful. How on earth did everyone know it was my birthday?"

"I think I said something," lied the vicar. He was suddenly sure Agatha Raisin was behind it and he was damned if he was going to let her take the credit. "Let's get all these parcels in."

Because the shops had been closed on Sunday, the presents were things like cakes and homemade jams.

The phone rang. Mrs. Bloxby answered it. It was Agatha to say happy birthday.

"The vicarage is full of flowers," said Mrs. Bloxby. "I feel like a film star."

Agatha's voice was suddenly sharp with concern. "Make sure all the bouquets are from the florist and no one has sneaked a homemade one in. Don't want you dying of wolfsbane."

When she rang off, Mrs. Bloxby told her husband what Agatha had said. They searched the bouquets, reading the cards, but all had come from the florist. "What a lot of thank you letters I am going to have to write," said Mrs. Bloxby.

The vicar realised for the first time that, even though it was morning, his wife looked tired.

"Look, someone's even sent a bottle of champagne. I'll open it now and then I'll help you open the presents. And I am taking you out for dinner tonight."

Mrs. Bloxby's eyes filled with tears. "You are so good to me, Alf. Isn't it too early for champagne?"

"Not on your birthday. I'll get the glasses."

In her office that morning, Agatha allocated jobs for the day. "You haven't got one for yourself," said Toni.

"I would like a quiet day so that I can go over my notes," said Agatha. The real truth was she wanted to be beside the phone in case Mark called. Of course, he could call her on her mobile number but Agatha was already fantasising about marrying him. Also, her secretary, Mrs. Freedman, had taken the day off to visit her niece.

When her detectives had left, Agatha discovered that Mrs. Freedman received quite a lot of phone calls. She longed to shout at callers to get off the line, but business was business, and so she settled down to take notes about missing pets, adulterous husbands and all the other bread and butter cases the agency dealt with. By three in the afternoon, she felt cross and hungry. She ordered a pizza to be delivered while she made herself yet another cup of black coffee.

Agatha had her mouth full of pizza when the phone rang. She picked it up. "Yes, may I help you?" she said, although because her mouth was full of pizza, it sounded more like, "Is, may elp yi."

"I would like to speak to Agatha Raisin." It was Mark. Agatha spat out her mouthful of pizza on the office floor.

"Mark!" she cooed. "It is Mark, isn't it?"

"Yes, Agatha. I wondered whether you would like to join me for dinner tonight?"

"That would be lovely," said Agatha. "What time and where?"

"The George. At eight o'clock?"

"Lovely. I'll see you there."

She had just replaced the receiver when Charles strode into the office.

"What are you doing here?" snapped Agatha.

"Why so hostile? Had a boring lunch with a cousin and thought I'd drop in on you."

"Well, I'm busy, so drop out."

Charles stared at the floor beside Agatha's desk. "Have you been sick?"

"No, it was too hot. I'll clean it up. I'm sorry, Charles, but I really am too busy."

"Who is he?" asked Charles.

"Who what?"

"You've got that travel bag of yours beside the desk, which usually means you plan to change into something slinky for a date. Good thing you didn't vomit pizza on it."

"You're talking rubbish. Oh, clear off. You make my head ache."

"Well, don't come crying to me if he turns out to be a rat."

Charles strolled off. Agatha cleaned the mess off the floor. The afternoon dragged on. Then one by one her detectives returned with their reports.

"I don't think any of this stuff warrants overtime," said Agatha. "So you can all go home."

"She's got a date," said Toni as she walked down the stairs from the office with Simon. "Any idea who it might be?"

"Not a clue. Anyway, whoever it is ought to be warned that our murderer might bump him off. Sometimes I think this murderer is out there, watching Agatha, and enjoying the fact that she hasn't got any idea who he is."

"I wonder if we should follow her, just to make sure she is safe," said Toni.

Simon laughed. "You would think we were talking about a wayward adolescent. She wouldn't thank us for interfering."

Agatha was ten minutes late arriving at the George. She had put on heavy make-up, wiped it off, tried again, decided that it was too little, and just as she decided she was happy with the result, a blob of mascara fell on her cheek and she had to start all over again.

She was wearing a scarlet chiffon jersey dress with a low neckline and scarlet red high-heeled shoes. A diamond pendant and little diamond earrings completed the ensemble.

Mark Dretter rose to meet her and Agatha suddenly felt very overdressed. The long French windows at the end of the restaurant were wide open because the evening was warm and humid. Mark was wearing a blue-and-white-checked shirt open at the neck. But he said, "You look magnificent."

"I had to deal with a very posh client before I came here," lied Agatha.

"Let's choose something to eat," said Mark, "and then you can tell me how you are getting on."

Agatha's bearlike eyes suddenly bored into him. "So that you can report to Gwen?"

He looked hurt. "Do you credit any man who invites you out for dinner as having an ulterior motive?"

"In my line of work, I'm suspicious of everyone," said Agatha. "Sorry."

"Never mind. What are you going to have to eat?"

Agatha had a healthy appetite but sadly knew that anything fattening seemed to go straight to her waistline. On the other hand, she told herself, she could start dieting the next day.

She ordered avocado stuffed with shrimp as a starter to be followed by steak and a baked potato. Mark said he would have the same and ordered a bottle of Macon to go with the meal.

"I can't help remembering having a meal here with David Herythe," said Agatha, "and then he ended up murdered. I hope I am not putting you in danger."

He laughed. "My sister is a security freak. My cottage has steel shutters on the downstairs windows, a CCTV camera over the door and burglar alarms back and front. Still, when you think about it, the murderer must have been following you. Just think. Might even be in this restaurant."

Agatha looked around the dining room. "They all look ordinary," she said. "Mind you, it's only after a murderer is caught that people say, look at those evil, staring eyes, or something like that, when in fact the murderer could be someone you would pass in the street without a second glance."

"Perhaps this murderer has given up," said Mark. "Have you got over that attempt on your life?"

"Of course," said Agatha, clasping her hands, which had begun to tremble, on her lap.

She privately thought that she would never forget Justin's attack. Her life had been threatened before and she had got over it quickly. Maybe she was suffering from an accumulation of attacks. Maybe she should get married and forget about being a detective. Maybe Dubai would be fun. She could play the hostess with the mostest at embassy parties. Would she have to wear a print dress and a large hat?

"Hullo!" said Mark. "I think you forgot I was here."

Agatha threw him a flirtatious look. "Now how could I forget such a handsome man?"

He smiled. "Easily, I should think. Why do you suspect Gwen?"

"Because her son, the baker, was serving up people in meat pies. There were the two of them living in that bakery. Don't tell me she didn't know what was going on."

"Mother love can be blind. Also, she wouldn't have

the strength. For example, you said that Tremund had been knocked on the head and pushed in the canal."

"I think it would be easy for such as Gwen Simple to enchant some man so that he would murder for her."

"But you told me the police had bugged her phone. She hasn't let anything slip. In fact, she leads a blameless life. Do eat your food. We've plenty of time to talk."

When she had finished her first course, Agatha said, "But you did think it might be a village murder and that the police are wasting their time looking at the Chicago end of the business."

"Just a feeling. Murder on such a scale would make anyone think it should be someplace like Birmingham rather than an English village. Anyway, what do you really know of that cleaner of yours?"

"Doris? Honest as the day is long."

"And Mrs. Tweedy?"

"She may be a bitch but she's pretty old."

"I bet there's someone in Carsely you haven't even thought of."

"I can't believe that," said Agatha. "Jill had consulting rooms in Mircester before she moved to the village. I wonder why she moved. More suckers to be found in a large town."

"Maybe one of her Mircester clients threatened her," said Mark. "Maybe that's why she moved. Oh, here's the steak."

Agatha was a fast eater. Mark, on the other hand, carefully cut off small pieces of steak one at a time and chewed them thoroughly before dissecting another bit.

"I'm tired of talking about murder," said Agatha. "Tell me about yourself."

"Not much to tell," he said, lifting a tiny piece of baked potato to his mouth. "Boring clerical work mostly. I might retire. There's a neighbour of yours called James Lacey. Writes books, doesn't he?"

"Yes, he's my ex."

"Didn't work out?"

"Obviously," said Agatha curtly.

"Well, I could do that. Write books, I mean."

"You'd need a private income."

"I have that."

Agatha's dream of Dubai faded. It wouldn't be the same, love in a cottage. She'd tried that with James.

"Could you possibly introduce me to James Lacey?"

"Yes, I can do that." Agatha was suddenly tired of his company. "Look, if we skip dessert and coffee, we can go now and catch him before he goes to bed."

As Mark talked enthusiastically to James about his ambition to write a book, Agatha gathered that Mark wanted to write any sort of book without knowing whether it was to be fiction or nonfiction. James found out that Mark's favourite reading was spy stories and suggested he could write one based on his experiences in Dubai. Agatha began to think there was something almost schoolboyish about Mark.

At last she yawned and said she had to go to bed. Mark reluctantly left with her and walked her to her cottage next door. To her irritation, Agatha recognised Charles's car.

"Are you going to invite me in?" asked Mark.

"Not tonight. I'm tired."

"We must do this again. I'll phone you." He kissed her warmly on both cheeks.

Agatha let herself into her cottage. Charles was asleep on the sofa with the cats on his lap. She glared at him and then went up to bed.

Would she really need to be in love with a man to get married to him? Mark was easy company. She paused. Where was the murderer now? Was she putting Mark in danger? And what about Charles and James? What about herself?

She opened her bedroom window and leaned out. A squat dark figure was just hurrying out of the lane. Agatha felt a spasm of pure dread. Whoever it was hadn't been walking a dog. There were only two cottages in Lilac Lane, her own and James's, and the lane ended at a field.

She rushed downstairs and shook Charles awake. "There was someone out in the lane," she said.

Charles straightened up, spilling cats onto the floor. "So what?"

"So what reason does anyone have for coming along here?"

He got to his feet. "I'll go and have a look."

"No!" screamed Agatha, hanging on to him. "I don't want to lose you."

He grinned. "This is so sudden." He planted a kiss on her nose. "I'll be careful."

Charles slipped on his shoes and went out into the lane. The air was damp and close and there was no moon. He ran lightly to the end of the lane. There was a streetlight at the corner. But it appeared the whole of Carsely had gone to sleep. Charles returned slowly to Agatha's cottage. He was worried about her. He had known Agatha to cope with murder and mayhem before and she always came bouncing back from every fright as good as new. But these murders were getting to her. She should get away on holiday and forget about the whole thing.

A pattering in the leaves of the lilac tree at the gate made him look up. Rain was beginning to fall.

"Anything?" demanded Agatha as he walked in.

"Nothing. Go to bed. You should go away somewhere, Aggie, and forget about the whole business. You're becoming a nervous wreck."

"I'm not going anywhere until I nail this bastard," said Agatha.

"Well, go to bed and we'll talk about it in the morning."

The grey, drizzly morning had a calming effect on Agatha. Horrors somehow seemed worse in bright sunlight. Charles was already up and on his way out. "Maybe see you later," he said.

Agatha had sometimes thought she might tell him she was turning the spare room into an office because she did not like the cavalier way he came and went in her life, but, she reminded herself, he had saved her life.

She decided to forget about the murders for the time being and concentrate on the work in hand. It was a busy week and the staff all worked hard. Agatha realised with delight that she would finally be able to give everyone a bonus and that news, delivered to her staff on Friday evening, was greeted with a great cheer. Agatha often worked on Saturdays with one other member of her staff, but decided that this time, as part of the celebration, they should all have the week-end off.

Agatha was sure Charles would have disappeared

again. She did not want to be alone and planned to leave her cottage and walk up to the pub. But as she arrived, she saw Roy Silver's car parked outside her door. She often viewed her former employee as an irritation. He was asleep at the wheel. She rapped on the window and he came awake with a start.

When he got out of the car, Agatha noticed that, for Roy, he was more soberly dressed than usual, wearing a business suit, but with a white shirt open at the neck, revealing enough gold chains to make an Indian woman's dowry.

"You've got to help me," he said as soon as he was out of the car.

"Come inside and tell me all about it," said Agatha. She wondered for a moment if Mark would phone and reminded herself she was not really interested in him.

The rain had stopped but the garden was still soaked. They sat in the living room. Roy asked for a vodka and tonic and Agatha helped herself to a gin and tonic.

"Now," she said. "What's up?"

"I was to handle the Leman account, you know, the Paris perfume people. Big promotion for their new perfume, Passion. Pedman gave it to that conniving bitch Maisie Byles." Pedman was Roy's boss.

"The wonderful world of public relations," said Agatha. "I'm glad to be out of it. Who the hell is Maisie Byles?"

"She only joined a month ago. Came from our rivals, JIG Publicity. Smarmed all over Mr. Pedman from day one."

"What does she look like?"

"Rabbity. Protruding eyes and big teeth."

"So how has she managed to charm Pedman?"

She found out the date of his little son's birthday and brought in a present. She offered to babysit when his babysitter let him down."

"JIG Publicity is a big powerful firm," said Agatha. "Why did she leave?"

"Don't know. She sneers at me."

"I've got a contact at JIG," said Agatha. "I'll see if I've got his home number."

She went to her desk, pulled out a drawer and lifted out a bulging address book.

"You must be the only person to still use an address book," commented Roy.

"Old numbers," said Agatha curtly. "Now what was his name? Maybe it's under JIG. Ah, here we are. Duncan Macgregor. Scottish as malt whisky. I'll phone him."

She rang a number and waited. Then she said, "No reply. I'll try his mobile."

This time Duncan answered. After the preliminary pleasantries, Agatha said, "What can you tell me about Maisie Byles?"

Roy waited impatiently, wishing he could hear what Duncan was saying.

At last, he heard Agatha say, "That's interesting. I'll bet Pedman didn't know anything about that."

She began to talk about her detective work, obviously in answer to Duncan's questions. Finally she rang off.

Agatha sat down and took a gulp of her drink and then said, "Maisie Byles left before she was pushed. She was handling Happytot baby formula. The silly cow went on her Facebook page and said that all mothers should be forced to breast-feed. Furious people at Happytot. JIG lost the account. Going to sack her but she cried and cried and said she had an invalid mother to support so instead they suggested she find other employment."

"Oh, dear," said Roy. "Do you think she has an invalid mother?"

"Not for a moment," said Agatha.

"So what do we do?" asked Roy.

"I'll send Pedman an e-mail and tell him all about it. If I do, are you sure you'll get the account?"

"Yes, it was initially offered to me but Maisie piped up and said surely it would be better if the account were handled by a woman."

"Okay, help yourself to another drink while I send this e-mail."

Agatha typed out an e-mail and sent it off.

218

"He always checks his e-mails, even at week-ends," said Roy. "Maybe he'll contact me."

"Let's hope so," said Agatha.

"So what's been happening in Murderville?" asked Roy.

"Quiet at the moment. I'm still sure Gwen Simple is behind it. Maybe she confessed to Jill Davent that she had helped her son with those murders."

"Oh, the Sweeney Todd case?"

"That's the one. Finish your drink and let's walk up to the pub and get something to eat. I don't feel like cooking."

"When did you ever cook, Agatha? You nuke everything in the microwave."

"Don't be rude. Let's go."

The pub was full inside but the tables and chairs outside had been wiped dry so they sat there and studied the menus, both finally settling for "sea fresh cod in golden crispy batter with hand-cut chips, mange tout and rocket from our own garden."

"They don't have a garden," said Agatha. "I hate rocket. Nasty, spidery vegetable."

Agatha lit a cigarette and blew smoke up towards the grey sky.

"Still smoking," said Roy. "It's so old-fashioned, Agatha."

"I suppose Maisie will now get the sack," said Agatha. "I must admit, that's a bit on my conscience."

"Don't worry. The cunning bitch insisted on a year's contract so Pedman is stuck with her. What if he's so enamoured of her that he does nothing?"

"He'll listen to me," said Agatha. "He'll be furious. He'll think the whole PR world is laughing at him. You know how hypersensitive he is." In the past, after she had sold her agency, Agatha had done PR work on a freelance basis for Pedman.

When their food arrived, Agatha noticed that the chips were the usual frozen ones. Between bites of food, she began to fret about the murders.

Said Roy, "Doris Simpson was one of her clients. Maybe she noticed another client, someone not on your list."

"I think she would have told me," said Agatha.

"Let's go and see her after we eat," urged Roy. "It'll take my mind off Pedman."

Doris welcomed them in. But when Agatha asked her if she had seen any other clients while she was there, Doris shook her head. "I did hear, however," said Doris, "that John Fletcher's missus had been to see her. You know, Rose Fletcher."

"And we've just come from the pub. Thanks, Doris. It's someone new."

"Won't she be working?" asked Roy as they made their way back to the pub.

"She works in the kitchen," said Agatha. "They don't serve meals after ten o'clock and it's now ten past. We should be able to have a word with her."

They went round to the kitchen door at the back of the pub. The door was standing open so they just walked in. Kitchen staff were clearing up, washing dishes and wiping down surfaces. Rose Fletcher was sitting at a table with a glass of beer in front of her.

"I want to ask you about Jill Davent," Agatha shouted above the kitchen noise.

"Outside with you," ordered Rose. "I'll talk to you outside."

Chapter Ten

Rose was a buxom woman with strong arms. She had dark brown curly hair and large brown eyes. "So?" she demanded.

"You were a client of Jill Davent, weren't you?" said Agatha.

"Yes."

"Is there anything you can tell me?" asked Agatha.

"Like what?"

"Did she try to blackmail you?"

"No," said Rose, "but she threatened to take me to court. I wouldn't pay her. I had a frozen shoulder. John told her about it. The next thing is she's round at the kitchen door saying she can cure it. So I made an appointment and went along. She fiddled about with a sort of massage. It took about five minutes or so. Then she demanded sixty pounds. My shoulder was as bad as ever so I told her to get lost.

"She said, 'I'll see you in the Small Claims Court.'

"I said, 'Why don't you do that? All your qualifications will be gone into.' She started screaming that it was dangerous to cross her. I walked away. I found an acupuncturist in Shipston-on-Stour and he was brilliant. I told everyone who would listen that she was a phony."

"When did this happen?" asked Agatha.

"The night before she was murdered."

"Did you see anyone else around?"

"Victoria Bannister. I bumped into her as I left. She was standing by the garden gate. I didn't think anything of it because Victoria was always spying on people."

"Did she say anything?" asked Agatha.

"No, she scurried off. Poor Victoria. Who would want to kill her?"

"She must have known something, or the murderer might have thought she knew something," said Agatha. "If you hear anything, Rose, let me know."

As they walked back to Agatha's cottage, Roy's mobile rang. He answered it and listened carefully. Agatha heard him say, "Yes, I'll be there tomorrow."

When he rang off, Roy did a little dance. "I've got it! I'm to be in Paris tomorrow."

"Good for you," said Agatha, but feeling suddenly low. Another week-end on her own. At her cottage, Roy said happily, "Good thing I left my travel bag in the car. Airport, here I come."

And not one word of thanks, thought Agatha as he sped off.

As she let herself into her cottage, the phone was ringing. She snatched it up. "Hi, Agatha," said Mark. "I might have found out something. All right if I call round?"

"Of course," said Agatha and ran up the stairs to her bathroom to remove the old make-up and put on a fresh layer.

Welcome to the maintenance years, thought Agatha, remembering the days of her youth when her legs felt like steel and her bras were usually limp disgraceful things because her breasts didn't need any support. Now it was all pelvic floor exercises, nonsurgical face-lifts, excruciating visits to the dentist to get the roots of her teeth cleaned, massage at Richard Rasdall's in Stow and all the other bits of hard work to keep age at bay.

She suddenly wondered why she was going to all this

trouble for a man she was not interested in, and changed into flat sandals and a blue cotton shift dress.

The bell rang as she was descending the stairs. When she opened the door, she was startled to realise she had forgotten that Mark was handsome.

Agatha led the way into the kitchen. "Take a seat," she said, "and tell me your news."

"I've been talking to Gwen," he said. "She and Jill were friends."

"That doesn't surprise me," said Agatha. "Criminals always feel comfortable in each other's company."

"Agatha! Gwen is a sweet woman and wouldn't harm a fly."

"Okay. Go on. What's the news?"

"Gwen says that Jill told her that someone had threatened to kill her."

"Yes, but who?"

"She couldn't find out."

Agatha sighed. "That doesn't get me any further."

"But don't you see? It must have been one of her clients in the village."

"Not necessarily," said Agatha. "It could have been her ex-husband. I can't believe that anyone in this village has the know-how to bug my cottage."

"But there are incomers to these Cotswold villages the whole time."

"I'll check it out with Mrs. Bloxby. But I feel sure

she would have told me if there was anyone new to the village that might fill the bill."

"I've got to dash," he said. "Maybe see you tomorrow?"

"Phone me," said Agatha.

He gave her a warm hug.

Well, well, well, thought Agatha, after he had left. It could work out. I could be Mrs. Dretter. I wish I could be married in white. I've always wanted a proper wedding. She glanced at the clock and judged it too late to call on Mrs. Bloxby and decided to see her after the church service.

Agatha really meant to go to the service but she slept late and only arrived at the church just as the service was finishing. Quite a large number of people began to stream out. Agatha waited patiently while Mrs. Bloxby talked to various villagers. At last she approached Agatha.

"Your husband's sermons seem to have become popular," commented Agatha.

"It's because he used the King James Bible and the old *Book of Common Prayer*," said Mrs. Bloxby. "People come from villages all around. The old language is so comforting in a world full of uncertainties. Would you like to come to the vicarage for coffee or something?"

"Yes," said Agatha. "I do need your advice."

"The signs are up for the Moreton Agricultural Show," said the vicar's wife. "Quite sad because it means that summer is over. I hope they get good weather for it. Some years, the field has been a sea of mud."

Agatha waited until they were both seated in the vicarage with glasses of sherry and said, "Mark Dretter called on me last night."

"The man from Dubai?"

"Yes, him. He keeps suggesting the murderer might be someone from the village. I said I didn't think there was anyone in Carsely with the expertise to bug my cottage and he said what about incomers. Know of anyone?"

"Only one fairly recent arrival, a Mr. Bob Dell."

"What does he do?"

"He is retired. I believe he was a banker. He wears frocks."

"He what?"

"He likes to dress as a woman."

"Why didn't I hear about this?" demanded Agatha. "A transvestite. It's a wonder he hasn't been driven away."

"As a matter of fact, he is popular. Even Alf has warmed to him because he brought armfuls of flowers to decorate the church. He contributes to all sorts of charities."

"Where does he live?"

"Badgers Loan. That Victorian villa, on Glebe Street at the back of the village store. It was owned by old Mrs. Dell, who died last year. She was ninety-four, very agile for her years. But her brain had begun to wander and she drove her motorised wheelchair right into the pond. She died of shock, they think. I'm surprised you didn't hear about it."

"I must have been away," said Agatha. "I think I'll call on this Bob Dell."

"You won't make remarks about his dress," cautioned Mrs. Bloxby.

"I," said Agatha Raisin, "am the soul of tact."

Bob Dell answered the door to her. He was a tall man in his sixties with a large nose and small mouth. He was wearing a blond wig and make-up and his thin body was draped in a long flower-patterned dress. Agatha introduced herself and he invited her in.

He led the way into a sitting room. The room was dominated by a grand piano covered with a fringed shawl. There were many photographs in silver frames on side tables and the floor was covered in a Persian rug. A stuffed owl in a glass case was placed in the middle of the room. One wall was lined with bookshelves. The three-piece suite was covered in bright chintz. Agatha sat down on the sofa and he lowered himself into an armchair facing her. He had forgotten to smooth the skirt of his dress under him and so he exposed a pair of long hairy legs in tights ending in white court shoes like sauce boats.

"Are you new to cross-dressing?" asked that soul of tact, Agatha Raisin.

"I only started last year," he said. "Why do you ask?"

"You haven't shaved your legs."

"I hate doing it. That's why I wear long dresses. Are you usually so rude?"

"Sorry. Just curious. You've heard about all those murders?"

"Yes, indeed."

"Know anything about electronics?"

"Can barely use the computer. I hate machines."

What you see is what you get, thought Agatha. This man is a gentle soul. But he needs help.

"Never economise on a wig," said Agatha. "That blond bird's nest you've got on your head screams fake. Phone up a firm called Banbury Postiche and get their catalogue. Aren't you getting a course of female hormones?"

"No, I'm new to all this. Are you usually so blunt?"

"Just trying to help. Where did you get that dress?"

"It was one of my mother's. She was very tall."

"Won't do. Wait a moment." Agatha took her iPad

230

out of her capacious handbag. "I'm just going to search for something. Ah, here we are. In Lower Oxford Street there's a shop called Trannies Delight. All sorts of clothes and things for people like you. I'll write it down."

"You are very kind. I'll go up to town tomorrow."

Agatha stood up. Having decided Bob could not possibly be the murderer, she was suddenly anxious to leave.

But she turned in the doorway and said, "Why a village like this? Wouldn't you be better off in London, where there must be lots of people like you?"

He smiled and said, "Oh, it would surprise you what you find in Cotswold villages. I am not alone."

Agatha walked away, feeling a cold breeze starting up. Soon it would be autumn. As she was turning the corner of Glebe Street, she suddenly froze. She sensed evil. She looked wildly around. Then she shrugged and walked on. Her near escape from death had left her nervous.

As she walked past the general store now closed for the Sunday afternoon, she had a sudden memory of visiting the Cotswolds as a child while her drunken parents in the grotty caravan they had borrowed from a friend bitched about how boring it all was. The child, Agatha, had found it enchanting. That was the start of her lifelong dream of living in the Cotswolds. But now there was a serpent in this Garden of Eden.

A brisk wind had sprung up, chasing the grey clouds above away to the east. In her cottage, she petted her cats and let them out into the garden and then checked her phone for messages. There was only one and it was from Mrs. Bloxby. "I forgot to remind you about the baking competition next Saturday," the vicar's wife said. "I know you will be too busy to contribute anything but there is a Sale of Work stall and I cannot get anyone to run it. Can you help?"

Agatha phoned her and said she would do it provided nothing came up to stop her attending. She was just wondering how to pass the rest of the day. She was sick and tired of studying all her notes on the murder cases.

There was a ring at the door. Agatha carefully looked through the spy hole first and saw Toni standing outside. She opened the door. "Come in. What brings you?" asked Agatha.

"Just a social call," said Toni. "I'm tired of going out on dates just to go out on dates, if you know what I mean. I hear you've got a new man in your life. Had dinner at the George."

"Oh, Mark Dretter. He's very handsome and I can't understand why I don't find him attractive. Want coffee?"

"Yes, please."

The doorbell rang again. "Help yourself," said Agatha, "while I see who's at the door."

It was Bill Wong. "What's happened?" demanded Agatha.

"Nothing," said Bill. "It's my day off and I thought I would look you up."

"Come into the kitchen. Toni's just arrived."

There was another ring at the doorbell. "If that's Simon, don't answer it," said Toni sharply. "He's started following me around again."

"Your car's outside and mine," said Agatha. "If it is him, I'll need to let him in."

But it was Phil Marshall. "I thought I'd see how you were bearing up," he said.

"Come in. Bill and Toni are in the kitchen."

Agatha reflected that nothing ever seemed to ruffle Phil. His gentle face and silver hair worked wonders at interviews. People always felt safe with him.

Toni made him a mug of coffee. "No breakthrough on the murders yet?" Phil asked Bill.

"Not a thing. What about you, Agatha?"

"Nothing."

"Wilkes had a mad hope we could pin all the murders on Justin and get the press off our backs, but at the time of Tremund's murder, for example, Justin was up in London working for a large company."

"What about Gwen Simple?" asked Agatha.

"Sorry. Nothing there. We're not even checking her phone calls now. Besides, she's alibied up to the hilt."

"I never thought she would murder people herself, but get someone to do it for her," said Agatha.

"Like her latest beau?"

"Who's that?" asked Agatha.

"A chap called Mark Dretter. Squeaky clean. On leave from the embassy in Dubai."

"He's not her beau," said Agatha. "He's been trying to help me with some detective work."

"Could've fooled me," said Bill. "They go everywhere together."

Agatha's face darkened. Had Mark only befriended her so that he could report to Gwen how she was getting on with trying to solve the murders?

"Anyway," she said huffily, "he's got some mad idea it might be someone in this village."

"Are there any weirdos in this village, Agatha?" asked Bill.

"Not that I know of. One cross-dresser but that's nothing these days."

"Oh, Bob Dell," said Phil. "It's odd. He wanted me to enlarge a photo of his niece. I often do some photo work for people in the village. I phoned him and said I was coming with it. I knocked and knocked but there was no reply."

"Did you see anyone around?" asked Agatha.

"Just some big old chap on a bike."

"I'm worried," said Agatha. "I'm going up there. He

didn't strike me as the sort of man to ask you to bring the photo and then not answer the door."

"I'll go," said Bill.

"I'll come with you," insisted Agatha. "The rest of you stay here."

"I'm sure we must be worrying about nothing," said Bill as he and Agatha hurried in the direction of Bob's home.

"All I would do is worry for the rest of the day," said Agatha stubbornly.

Glebe Street looked innocent and quiet. Agatha rang the bell beside the door of Bob's villa. There was no reply. "Phil said something about knocking," said Bill. "Maybe the bell doesn't work."

He hammered on the door.

A little breeze rustled through a clematis beside the door and then died away.

"See if you can open the door," urged Agatha.

Bill tried the doorknob. "Locked," he said.

"Break in!" said Agatha.

"I can't. I haven't a warrant. Let's try round the back. He may be in the garden."

They walked along a path at the left side of the villa. The garden was a profusion of flowers. On the patio was a garden table with a half-finished glass of wine and a book, its pages fluttering in the breeze. Draped over a chair by the table was a paisley shawl.

Agatha cupped her hands and peered in the French windows. It was the room she had sat in with Bob.

"Can you see anyone?" asked Bill.

"No one."

"We'll try later," said Bill. "I'm sure you're worried about nothing."

Agatha would not give up. Her breath had steamed up the glass. She wiped it with a handkerchief and peered in again. Then she tried the handle on the window.

"It's open," she said, and before Bill could stop her, she went into the room, calling, "Bob! Are you there?"

There was a faint sound from behind the sofa. Agatha peered over and then shrieked, "Bill!"

Bob Dell lay on the floor. His face was a mass of blood.

Bill hurried in and knelt beside him. "His pulse is faint." He phoned for an ambulance and then called police headquarters.

Toni and Phil had heard the sirens and hurried up to Glebe Street to find Bob Dell being loaded into an ambulance. Toni was worried about Agatha because Agatha's face was chalk white.

"I think you should go to the hospital as well, Agatha," said Toni. "You've had a bad shock."

"I'll be all right," said Agatha. "I feel it's got something to do with my visit to him."

Wilkes came up to Agatha. "You may go home, Mrs. Raisin, and we'll be with you shortly to take a statement."

"Look at them!" said Agatha, pointing to the forensic team, who were about to enter the villa. "Masks, heads covered, suited up, little booties. If they were on television they would have shoulder-length hair and stilettos on."

"Come along," urged Toni, putting an arm around Agatha's waist.

Back in Agatha's cottage, Toni tried to persuade her to drink hot sweet tea but Agatha stubbornly demanded gin and tonic. "You don't have any ice," said Toni.

"Snakes and bastards! Who cares?" yelled Agatha.

Toni reluctantly fixed a gin and tonic. Agatha gulped it down and demanded another. "Don't you think you ought to wait until after you've made your statement?" said Toni.

"No, I do not!"

To Toni's relief, Agatha was still relatively sober when Wilkes and a detective Agatha did not recognise came to take her statement. Then Phil was questioned and explained that he had seen a heavyset man leaving Glebe Street on a bike. "I didn't get a good look at him," said Phil apologetically. "He had a baseball cap pulled down over his face. He was wearing grey trainers and a grey zip-up jacket. He had gloves on his hands."

"We can only hope Mr. Dell survives the attack and can tell us who did this to him," said Wilkes.

"Make sure there's a police guard outside his hospital room," said Agatha.

"Don't tell me how to do my job," snapped Wilkes. "You're like the bloody angel of death, you are. Report to headquarters in the morning and we'll have your statement printed out and ready for you to sign. The same goes for you, Mr. Marshall."

After they had left, Toni said to Phil, "Would you wait with Agatha? I'll go home and pack a bag. I think I should stay with her this evening."

"I'll be all right," said Agatha.

"You'll do as you're told for once in your bossy life," said Toni.

"Then get me another G and T before you go."

"Off you go, Toni," said Phil. "I'll get it."

When Phil returned to the kitchen with Agatha's drink, she was hugging herself and shivering. "It's so cold," she moaned.

"You're in shock. Upstairs to bed with you."

Agatha drained the gin and tonic in one gulp and then allowed Phil to lead her upstairs. She sat groggily on the edge of the bed while Phil removed her shoes. Then he managed to get her under the duvet and switched on the electric blanket.

When he finally went downstairs again, he reflected that he had never seen Agatha in such a state of shock before. There was something about these murders that had got to her. Phil felt he owed a great debt to Agatha. Who else would have recognised his talent as a photographer and employed a man like himself in his late seventies?

He decided to phone Charles. Agatha had a list of numbers pinned up next to the phone. There were two numbers for Charles: his home phone and his mobile. Beside the mobile number, Agatha had scribbled, *Never answers*.

He phoned the home number. Charles's gentleman's gentleman, Gustav, answered the phone. He asked who Phil was and what was his business.

Phil said he was phoning because Agatha Raisin was in dire need of help. "I am afraid," said Gustav, "that Sir Charles is unavailable," and rang off.

Gustav jumped nervously when Charles came up behind him and asked, "Who was on the phone?"

"Someone selling double glazing," said Gustav. He detested Agatha and often feared that his boss might marry her.

Charles was aware that Gustav's eyes had a way of rolling up to the ceiling when he was lying. "So what does Agatha want?" he demanded. "Tell the truth or you can kiss your bonus goodbye."

"She's always bothering you," protested Gustav. "It was some man called Marshall said she was in need of help."

Phil was relieved when Toni and Charles arrived at the same time. Charles was told everything that had been happening and how they were frightened that Agatha was cracking up under the strain.

Now that Agatha was being monitored, Phil decided to go to his home in the village. Charles watched Toni fidgeting around and then asked, "What's up?"

"I had a date for tonight but I cancelled it."

"Not one of your old men?" asked Charles, knowing Toni's penchant for dating older men.

"No, he's a medical student. Only a few years older than me. He's nice."

"Phone him up and uncancel," said Charles. "It doesn't take two of us to baby-sit."

Agatha awoke an hour later. Her head ached and her mouth felt dry. Poor Bob Dell, she thought. Then she suddenly sat up in bed. What was it that Bob had said as she had left? *I am not alone.*

Did that mean someone else in this village was masquerading as a woman?

She slowly got up, her mind racing. Charles heard her moving about and came upstairs. "You look a wreck," he said heartlessly.

She clutched his shoulders. "Have you heard what happened to Bob Dell?"

"Yes. Bill Wong called when you were asleep. Poor Bob died in hospital an hour ago."

"Oh, how awful. But there's something else. He was a cross-dresser. When I wondered why he didn't choose to live in a town where he might meet more of his own kind, he said, 'I am not alone.'"

"So?"

"So maybe there's someone in this village that everyone thinks is a woman."

"You smell of old gin, sweetie. Have a shower and come downstairs and eat something."

When Agatha finally appeared, washed and wearing a change of clothes, she looked like her old self.

"I'm making you tea and toast," said Charles. "No more booze for you."

"I'd like a large glass of mineral water," said Agatha. "I've got a mouth like a gorilla's armpit."

"You do have a way with words. All right. One glass coming up. But eat some toast."

"Who could it be?" fretted Agatha. "I must look at my notes."

"Toast and tea first. Notes afterwards."

Agatha dutifully ate two slices of buttered toast washed down with tea. "Rats! It can't be Gwen Simple."

"No," agreed Charles. "Much as you'd like to think so. Who else is there?"

"Let's go and ask Mrs. Bloxby."

"It's getting late, Agatha."

"It's only ten o'clock."

"Still, leave the woman alone until tomorrow. And I gather from Phil that you've got to go to headquarters in the morning to sign a statement. The best thing," said Charles, "is that you put the whole thing out of your head and we'll watch something stupid and easy on television. Give your mind a rest."

They watched *NCIS* although Agatha complained that the scriptwriters obviously had a father complex as it was yet another story with one of the characters having trouble with his father. Then they watched an old

Jackie Chan movie until Charles fell asleep and Agatha took herself off to bed.

She set the alarm. She was sure she would not sleep and was surprised to be awakened in the morning by the alarm.

When she went downstairs, she found Charles awake, dressed and waiting for her. "I'll drive you in to headquarters," he said. "You're liable to think of someone, shout 'Eureka!' and drive into a lamppost."

At police headquarters, Charles waited while Agatha was led away to sign her statement for Bill Wong.

"That'll be all," said Bill. "You should take the day off, Agatha. Why are you staring at me like that?"

"You checked out the backgrounds of all the people who you knew were Jill's clients?"

"Of course."

"What about Mrs. Tweedy?"

Chapter Eleven

Agatha, you need a rest," said Bill. "You surely don't suspect that old woman?"

"Listen to me. Bob Dell was a cross-dresser. When I wondered why he had chosen to live in a village instead of a town where there would be more of his own kind, he said, 'I am not alone.'"

Bill laughed. "And so you immediately leap to the conclusion that Mrs. Tweedy is a murderous transvestite?"

"Humour me, Bill. What's her story?"

"She's from a village in Oxfordshire called Offley

Crucis. She moved to Oxford and then Carsely a year ago after a tragedy."

"What tragedy?"

"Her twin brother was killed in a fire."

"How did the fire start?"

"Faulty electrics. Really, Agatha, we've gone into everyone's background thoroughly."

"What happened to Mr. Tweedy?"

"There isn't one. She said she just called herself Mrs because she didn't want to be damned as the village spinster."

"No one talks about spinsters anymore," said Agatha. "She may be old but she looks powerful and she's got strong hands."

"You've been working too hard, Agatha. Let it go."

"Agatha," protested Charles, "we can't go calling on Mrs. Tweedy and accuse her of being a man."

"I want to go to Offley Crucis where she lived, and find out about this twin brother. What if she wanted to inherit the lot and to take his identity as well?"

Charles sighed. "Can we eat first?"

"The nearest greasy spoon on the road will do."

Agatha phoned her office and said she was taking the day off. Then she and Charles set out, stopping at a roadside restaurant for a full English breakfast and several cups of coffee.

Offley Crucis turned out to be a very small village at the end of a one-track road. The weather had turned fine again. There were a few redbrick houses clustered around a pond. There was a small church and a general store. Apart from a few ducks bobbing about the pond, nothing moved.

"Pity there isn't a pub," said Charles. "I hate the idea of knocking on doors."

"I hope there are some people at home," said Agatha. "It's quite near Oxford and could be one of those sort of dormitory villages. Oh, look! That woman's just come out into her front garden. I'll try her."

"I'll leave you to it," said Charles lazily.

He sat on a bench by the pond and watched as Agatha entered into animated conversation with the woman. She came back and said, "That's a bit of luck. She's new to the village but she says if we go to the pub at the next village, Sipper Magna, we'll find an old boy who is a fund of gossip. His name is Barney Gotobed."

At the pub, they were told they would find Mr. Gotobed at "his" table in the garden by the cedar tree.

Agatha, who had expected to find a sort of local

yokel was surprised to find an elderly, scholarly looking gentleman in a worn tweed jacket and flannels. He had thinning grey hair and bright intelligent eyes.

Introducing herself and Charles, Agatha said, "Mind if we join you and ask some questions about the Tweedys?"

"Please do," he said. "You may call me Barney. I seem to have acquired a reputation for being the local gossip."

They pulled up chairs and sat down. "We're curious about the fire in which the brother died," said Agatha. "May we get you another drink?"

"A lager would be fine."

"Could you get it, Charles?" said Agatha. "And a gin and tonic for me."

Charles went off reluctantly. Then he came back. "I seem to have forgotten my wallet, Agatha."

"As usual," grumbled Agatha, getting out her wallet and handing him a twenty-pound note.

"So what about the fire?" asked Agatha eagerly.

"Anthony and Lavender Tweedy were twins," he began, leaning back in his chair. "Could hardly tell them apart because Lavender dressed like a man. They hated each other and lived separate lives in the same house. They had it altered, you know, so each had separate kitchens and bathrooms. Neither of them had ever had a job. The parents had been extremely wealthy; old

Mr. Tweedy owned several storage unit sites and had invested cleverly. They died when the twins were at Oxford, I believe. A car crash on the M5. To everyone's surprise, the twins chucked up their studies and returned home and there they stayed for years and years until the fire. I suppose no one thought much of it. Every village has its eccentrics. I said they didn't work? That's not quite true. Anthony was clever on the stock exchange and increased their wealth considerably. Somehow, much as he openly loathed his sister, they had joint accounts and shared the money."

Charles came back with the drinks.

"And the fire?" asked Agatha.

"The pair of them were great readers and the house was like a library. I think that's why it was such an awful blaze. It went up like a torch. Lavender was found in the garden suffering from smoke inhalation and cuts where she had smashed a window and jumped out."

"That's odd," said Agatha. "Couldn't she just have run out of the door?"

"They were both afraid of burglars and the windows were all locked and sealed. It was Anthony's job to lock the doors at night and he kept the keys in his room. Also he kept his part of the house locked. Added to that, the pair of them considered bottle gas more economical and stored several canisters and so they all exploded. The nearest fire station is some miles away and by the time they arrived, it was too late. All that was left of Anthony, I gather, were charred remains."

"Any suggestion that the fire had been deliberately started?" asked Agatha.

He raised his eyebrows. "Do you mean, did Lavender deliberately try to get rid of her brother?"

"Could be."

"The insurance company did a full investigation. It was an early Georgian house and the fire was judged to be the result of an electrical fault."

"Did you ever talk to the Tweedys?" asked Charles.

"They barely spoke to anyone. People pretty much ignored them. They became part of the village scenery."

"But you were interested in them," said Agatha.

"Since I retired from Oxford University, I found I liked studying people and speculating about them. I suppose that's how I got my reputation as a gossip. What is your interest in the Tweedys? Is it anything to do with all these murders?"

"Mrs. Tweedy was a client of that therapist who was murdered," said Agatha. "I'm just checking up on everyone."

Said Barney, "Lavender Tweedy consult a therapist? I find that very hard to believe unless she has changed considerably."

"What if she had some awful secret and she just had

to tell someone?" said Agatha. "And what if that someone was a blackmailing therapist?"

"From what I remember of Lavender, she wouldn't have confided in anyone," said Barney.

"And the fire was really an accident?" asked Agatha.

"Yes, of course. Faulty wiring. It was an old house. A developer bought the ruin, knocked it down and built a couple of villas. There was a good bit of land, you see."

"Can you remember the name of the insurance company?" asked Agatha.

Barney grinned. "You do have a nasty suspicious mind. Falcon Insurance in Cheltenham. I remember the name clearly because there was an investigator down here for quite a time."

"This really is one of your more dramatic flights of fancy," grumbled Charles as they got in the car and Agatha announced they were going to Cheltenham.

"I've got to follow this up," said Agatha. "I've got nothing else."

Cheltenham Spa in Gloucestershire has some fine Regency buildings. It has recently changed from a genteel town, famous for retired colonels and their ladies and has become a rougher place. But it still has the pump room and beautiful gardens and those magnificent terraces of white houses. Although inland, it has the air of a seaside town and one almost expects to turn a corner and see a pier.

Falcon Insurance was situated in one of these mansions. They were passed from secretary to secretary until they were told that a Mr. Brian Dempsey would see them.

Brian Dempsey was a tired-looking grey man: grey suit, grey face, grey hair.

"I investigated the Tweedy fire," he said. "I was very thorough. Of course, all those canisters of butane gas had helped to burn everything to a crisp. The body of Anthony Tweedy was just a scorched mess."

Charles said, "I heard it is quite easy to fake an electric fault. Shred a bit of wire and put a lit book of matches next to it and clear off."

"How much was the house insured for?" asked Agatha.

"Eight hundred thousand."

They were sitting in easy chairs in a well-appointed office. Agatha suddenly sat up straight, her eyes dilated. Charles thought she ought to have a lightbulb above her head.

"The body was that of Anthony Tweedy was it?" she asked.

"Who else could it be?" Brian said. "Lavender identified what was left by the remains of his watch and one of his handmade shoes had escaped most of the burning."

"So no dental records? No DNA?"

Brian said testily, "I am very good at my job. I spent a lot of time making sure the fire was accidental. What the hell are you getting at?"

"The brother and sister hated each other," said Agatha. "Get a load of this. What if—just what if—the body was that of Lavender, not Anthony?"

Brian laughed. "You must realise, I interviewed Lavender. One very distressed old lady. I'm not a fool, you know. Also, she was the spitting image of a photograph she showed me."

"But they were identical twins," protested Agatha.

Brian rose to his feet as a signal that the interview was over. "It's been very interesting to meet you, Mrs. Raisin," he said. "Ever thought of writing detective fiction?"

"Don't be rude," said Agatha. "Come along, Charles."

"I could do with a drink," said Charles when they left the building. "I want you to sit down and tell me exactly what's got into that crazy head of yours."

They headed for the bar of the Queen's Hotel. "It's like this," said Agatha, taking a gulp of gin and tonic. "Bob Dell was a cross-dresser. He said he wasn't alone. Right? What if one transvestite recognised the man behind so-called Lavender Tweedy's disguise? What if the Tweedy woman saw me going there and got worried?"

"Well," said Charles cautiously, "what on earth can you do about it?"

"Teeth often survive a fire. I wonder if the body was buried? I should talk to Bill."

"And he will consult his superiors and Wilkes will tell you to stop interfering in police business."

"I wonder what's in the Tweedy garden?"

"Agatha, the police searched all the gardens looking for wolfsbane."

"Snakes and bastards. And it could all have been uprooted."

"What about the allotments?"

The allotments were those strips of land just outside Carsely rented by various villagers to grow vegetables and flowers.

"I seem to remember they searched those as well," said Agatha gloomily.

"Just suppose I go along with this mad idea of yours," said Charles. "Could she have got an allotment in a nearby village? Mrs. Bloxby would know if there were any available."

Agatha's face cleared. "Let's go and ask!"

Mrs. Bloxby's gentle face looked bewildered as Agatha poured out her new theory and then demanded to know if Mrs. Tweedy could have rented an allotment in any nearby village.

"Do have another scone, Sir Charles, while I think," said Mrs. Bloxby. "I'll ask Alf."

She went along to her husband's study but unfortunately left the door open. "You mean that pesky woman is here again?" they heard the vicar demand. "Hasn't she got a home of her own to go to?" Then the study door was shut.

Charles grinned. "Doesn't like you much, does he?"

"That man is not a Christian," snapped Agatha.

Mrs. Bloxby came back. "There is a village called Upper Harley. It's about ten miles from Carsely. They had allotments available last year. It's little more than a hamlet so they might allow outsiders to rent."

"I'll go over there tonight," said Agatha. "Don't want to be snooping around in the daytime."

"I can't come with you," said Charles. "Got a dinner engagement. You'd better take someone with you."

"I'll think about it," said Agatha.

"Don't be silly," snapped Charles. "There's nothing to think about. Don't go alone."

That evening, Charles talked politely at dinner while all the time his mind raced. Damn, Agatha. If her mad conjectures were right, she was putting herself in serious danger. He looked anxiously at the fading light of the evening beyond the long windows of the dining room. It would be dark soon.

At last he couldn't bear it any longer. He made a muttered excuse and found his way to the lavatory. He sat down on the pan, took out his phone, where he had all the numbers of Agatha's detectives listed. He rapidly told them where Agatha was going and begged them all to get over there. Then he phoned Bill Wong and managed to get him at home. Bill listened in amazement as Charles rapidly told him about Agatha's theory and where she had gone.

"I think that attack on her life upset her," said Bill, "or she would never have come up with this load of rubbish."

"There's something awfully convincing about it," pleaded Charles. "Can't you just get out to that allotment and check?"

"It's my night off," protested Bill. "Oh, all right. But I am really going to give her a blast."

As soon as it was dark, Agatha set out, listening to the irritating voice on her sat-nav directing her to Upper Harley. Despite the Cotswolds being such a tourist attraction, there are little Cotswold villages like Upper Harley, buried away in the wolds and seldom visited.

She kept checking in her rearview mirror to make sure she wasn't being followed, but there were several cars behind her until she swung off the main road. Her way took her down dark twisting lanes where overhanging trees blotted out the moon.

Finally she arrived, parked in the centre and got out and looked around. Upper Harley appeared to consist of a huddle of houses beside a pond. There was no evidence of a shop or pub. Agatha marched up to the nearest house and knocked on the door, demanding to know where the allotments were. "No use you wanting one," said the woman who answered the door. "Thems bin sold off for housing."

Agatha's heart sank, but she pursued with, "Where are they anyway?"

"You come by car?"

"Yes."

"Take that liddle lane t'other side of the pond. Drive slow, mind. Do be sheep sometimes. Quarter mile up on the left."

Agatha thanked her. Got into her car and drove slowly off, hoping the sheep would have gone to sleep.

There were no trees over the lane and she was grateful for the bright moonlight, thinking that otherwise she might have missed the allotments, hidden as they were behind a straggly hedge. It was only when she was driving at a snail's pace and coming to a break in the hedge that she noticed through the back a few strips of land. She collected her camera and a powerful torch and made her way through the gap.

Because, probably, of the incipient sale, many of the former allotments had been left to run wild. But there were a few sheds and a few cultivated strips. One had beans, another marrows, but Agatha was looking for flowers.

A little wind sprang up, making urgent whispering sounds. Agatha suddenly wanted to forget the whole thing and go home. She wished she had brought Toni or Simon with her. She realised dismally that for once her nerves were in bad shape.

Telling herself severely not to be such a wimp, she made her way carefully past the beds, shining her torch to left and right. At the far wall, she saw a shed behind a garden strip of flowers: hollyhocks, late roses and some early chrysanthemums. She shone the torch over the flowers. No wolfsbane. Time to go home. She was about to turn around when Agatha saw a gleam of glass behind the shed. She made her way round and found a small greenhouse. The door was padlocked. Agatha shone her torch in the window.

The beam picked out a healthy clump of what she recognised to be wolfsbane.

She grinned in triumph and took out her phone to call the police.

That was when a heavy blow from a spade struck her right on the back of the head and she slumped down on the ground.

Agatha fought desperately against the blackness trying to engulf her. Above her, she heard a sneering voice say, "You interfering old cow. I enjoyed watching you bumbling around. You're cleverer than I thought. So you just lie there while I dig you a nice grave."

Agatha's head swam. She's going to bury me alive, she thought. Let her think I'm unconscious. Or is it him? I bet it's that brother, Anthony.

She could hear sounds of digging. Blood from the wound on her head was seeping into her eyes as she made an effort to see if she could move. But that was when her strength failed her and she blacked out.

Bill and Alice Peterson were racing through the night. Bill ruefully had to admit to himself that he had been glad of the distraction. He had long fancied Detective

Alice, although relationships with colleagues were frowned on. Nonetheless, he had invited her home for supper, but his mother had been singularly rude, not that Bill saw it as such because he adored his mother and thought she was perhaps not feeling well.

"Do you really think Agatha might be onto something?" asked Alice.

"Not for a moment," said Bill. "This is just one very far-fetched idea."

"She's come up with far-fetched ideas before," said Alice.

"But this one's a stinker. Don't worry. We'll sort her out and have a coffee on the road back."

They had just parked outside the allotments when another car drew in behind them and Toni and Simon got out.

"Charles really panicked," said Bill. "Come on, you two. Let's get it over with and we can all go home."

They walked into the allotments, all shouting "Agatha!" at the tops of their voices.

A man emerged from a shed and shouted, "Wot you bleeding lot doing, stomping my prize marrows? I'll 'ave the law on yer."

"We're looking for a friend," said Bill.

"Ud that be old Mrs. Tweedy?"

Bill froze for a moment. "Where's her allotment?"

"Up back. But you're going to pay for that marrow wot you stood on."

They hurried up, Bill and Alice shining their torches. They came across a deep hole in the ground. With a spasm of terror, Bill shone his torch into it and saw, under a pile of earth, a woman's foot sticking out.

He shouted to Alice to phone headquarters and get help, and then he and Simon eased themselves down into the hole and frantically began to clear the earth away from the body underneath until Agatha was revealed, her face covered in blood.

He felt her neck. "There's a pulse," he said. "I daren't move her. Toni, there's some of that silver stuff we use for shocked people in the back of my car. Get it and we'll wrap her up until the ambulance comes."

A voice behind him made him jump. "Is she dead?" Charles stood there, his face white in the moonlight.

"No, but she's in a bad way," said Bill.

"Where's the Tweedy woman—or man, if Agatha's got it right?"

"We haven't had time to look. But Alice has phoned headquarters. They'll be a nationwide search for her."

Villagers had got wind of a fuss up at the allotments. Alice got police tape out and cordoned off the area. The marrow man was driven outside, still grumbling about his prize vegetables.

To Bill's immeasurable relief, an air ambulance helicopter soared round overhead and landed in the field opposite. Paramedics came rushing up with a stretcher.

Unconscious, Agatha was lifted up and taken to the helicopter. Charles was allowed to go with her, but Toni and Simon were told to wait behind until their statements were taken.

The surgeons estimated that Agatha's thick hair had saved her skull. When she recovered consciousness, Agatha found Bill and Inspector Wilkes beside her bed.

She gave a feeble grin. "So I'm alive?"

"We would like to take a few notes," said Wilkes. Then, as if it were being forced out of him, he said, "That was a good piece of detective work. Tell me how you figured it out."

In a weak voice, Agatha told him about meeting Bob Dell and how his remark about not being alone and his subsequent murder had started her to think of Mrs.— or as they now suspected—Mr. Tweedy. But soon her eyes closed and she fell asleep.

The next day, she was stronger and able to give a full account. When she had finished, Mrs. Bloxby came in, her kind face creased with worry. "I should never have told you about those allotments," she said.

"Just as well you did," said Agatha. "Is there a police guard on my room?"

"Of course. They haven't caught Tweedy yet."

"I bet they've been too slow to freeze the bank accounts. He could be anywhere."

"Why did we never think Mrs. Tweedy might be a man?" asked the vicar's wife.

Agatha sighed. "She appeared old and rude. Some old people lose sexuality or femininity, or whatever and people never really look at them properly. I wish they would catch her. And how did a woman who'd never had a job know how to bug my cottage? Oh, I suppose it was easy with all those little gadgets you can buy. Once she'd got in, all she had to do was spread them around. I keep saying 'she.'"

Agatha looked around the room. "No flowers?"

"Hospitals don't allow flowers these days," said Mrs. Bloxby. "People have sent chocolates, fruit and cakes but the police took them all away for forensic examination in case they contained poison."

"Where's James?"

"He's in Thailand, but he phoned to find out about you. The press have been trying to get in to see you."

"Do you know," said Agatha wearily, "I can't for once face them. And look at my poor head! All done up in bandages and shaved underneath. I'll need to wear a wig until it grows back in again."

The door opened and Charles came in carrying a brown paper bag, which he dumped on the table in front of Agatha. "Double cheeseburger, chips and coffee," he said.

"You're an angel," cried Agatha. "The hospital food is rubbish."

"Oh, Sir Charles," protested Mrs. Bloxby. "Couldn't you have brought something a little healthier?"

"She thrives on junk food," said Charles. "Look, Aggie, you'd better clear off on holiday somewhere when you get out of here."

"Nonsense. The solving of this case will bring the agency a lot of work. Can't wait to get back."

But worried Mrs. Bloxby noticed that the well-manicured hands holding the cardboard container of coffee trembled a little.

After two weeks, and on Agatha's last day in hospital, Bill Wong called to say that the body of the supposed Anthony had been exhumed and it had been established that it was in fact the sister, Lavender, who had perished and that Anthony had taken her identity.

"I'm surprised there was enough left to get DNA," said Agatha.

"Enough in a surviving molar," said Bill.

No one had told Agatha that her police guard had

been told not to allow Roy Silver admittance, everyone being annoyed that he had arrived as soon as the attempt on Agatha's life had reached the newspapers, because he had held press conferences on the steps of the hospital, bragging about how he helped Agatha with her cases. All her detectives had called daily with their reports. Charles and Mrs. Bloxby would have liked to keep them away but Agatha insisted on being kept up to date.

When she got home, Doris Simpson was waiting with her cats and watched anxiously as Agatha petted them and then burst into tears.

"Now, now, my love," said Doris. "You've got to take it easy."

"Sure," said Agatha, mopping her eyes. "I'll be all right in a day or two."

"That wicked man won't dare to come near you," said Doris.

"I hope not," said Agatha. "I suppose he didn't bump me off at the beginning because he thought I was a fool. He must have told Jill Davent something and she tried to blackmail him and set all the murders in motion. They do say that after the first murder, the others come easy."

Charles was hosting the annual village fete on the grounds of his estate. He felt his face stiff with smiling and he was bored to tears. At the end of the day, he retreated into his house and into his study while Gustav brought him a beer. He put his feet up and then remembered he had bought a lottery scratch card for a pound. He fished it out of his pocket along with a coin and began to scratch busily. He could hardly believe his eyes. It appeared he had won seven hundred and fifty thousand pounds. Found money, he thought. This demands a special treat.

Then he thought of Agatha. She badly needed a holiday. What if he bought her one? What kind of holiday would she feel compelled to take? But the elderly aunt who lived with him and Gustav should have something. He called them in.

Gustav wanted a new motorbike and his aunt wanted a big donation to a cancer society. When Gustav had left to pore over catalogues, Charles asked his aunt, "I'd like to send Agatha Raisin on holiday, a holiday she can't refuse. Any ideas?"

"Oh, that Miss Marple of yours. What about the *Orient Express* to Venice?"

"Brilliant!"

It almost didn't happen because the day after, Charles's stinginess took over. The upkeep of the estate swallowed money and he was already regretting his generosity. But he could hardly tell his aunt or Gustav that he had changed his mind. The *Orient Express* would be expensive. On the other hand, he thought Agatha was a nervous wreck, and he wanted the old Agatha back to amuse him. Still, he thought hopefully, maybe she'll turn it down.

Epilogue

At long last, after a month, Agatha decided to accept Charles's offer and, for once, all her friends were glad to see her go. She had been snappish and irritable, throwing herself into her work, slaving away long hours, and refusing all social invitations. Bill Wong had pleaded with her to go to Victim Support, which got the furious reply, "There is nothing up with me."

It was almost as if Agatha felt that living in some sort of perpetual rage might keep her fear of Anthony Tweedy coming back to murder her at bay.

Concerned for her welfare, Charles had hired a limo

driver, an ex-member of the police force, Dave Tapping, to take her to Victoria Station in London. He was a powerful-looking man and Charles felt reassured that Agatha would have a bodyguard as well as a driver.

On the road to London, Dave talked amiably about the family holiday he had just returned from in Florida with his wife, Zoe, and his two children, Harry and Hannah. He broke off as Agatha began to cry and handed her a pile of tissues. Agatha had suddenly been overwhelmed with regret that she had never managed to get married to some sensible man and have children.

"George Clooney's getting married in Venice," said Dave, trying to cheer her up. "Is that why you're crying?"

Agatha gave a reluctant laugh. "Not one of my fantasies," she said.

At Victoria, she asked Dave if he would mind parking the car and walking her to the Pullman train, which was to be her transport for the first part of her journey. She was to join the *Orient Express* at Calais.

As she settled in the dining car, Agatha thought bitterly that she must face up to the fact that she had lost her nerve and that her days of detecting were over.

But the smooth rolling of the train and a superb meal slowly roused her spirits.

At Folkstone, the passengers were met by a traditional jazz band. One matron, carried away, was bopping to the music. Oh dear, thought Agatha, Middle England out to play.

Then they were informed that because of a French rail strike, they were all to board buses to take them across the Channel by the tunnel and on to Arras, halfway to Paris. The bus was one of those with tables to seat four without enough leg room.

By the time Agatha got to Arras, she was feeling tired and grumpy but was mothered by an efficient French steward into her little cabin on the *Orient Express*. She settled for the late dinner at ten in the evening and began to unpack a few things, including a black velvet dress for dinner because formal dress was mandatory. It was a beautiful train, all shining wood and inlaid marquetry. The lavatory was at the end of the corridor, a large room and the toilet had an old-fashioned pump.

When she reached the dining room that evening, she wished she had gone for an earlier meal because the liquored-up pseuds were out in force, talking in loud baying voices, trying to outposh each other. But the food, even to Agatha's not very sophisticated palate, seemed to be the best she had ever tasted. For the first time, she began to relax and hard on the heels of that relaxation came the guilty feeling that she had been rude to her helpful friends and had not thanked Charles enough.

In her compartment was a little pile of free postcards with an instruction just to hand them to the steward for posting. Before she went to bed, Agatha wrote to Charles, Mrs. Bloxby and her detectives, thanking them all for their concern and saying she missed them.

In the morning, she raised the blind. Outside was a panorama of the Swiss Alps and Lake Geneva, benign in the sun. Agatha's heart rose and with it her hopes. Perhaps in Venice she might meet some handsome man. She settled down to enjoy the rest of the journey.

At Venice, an *Orient Express* helper led them off the train and there was a long wait while all the luggage and passengers going to all the different hotels were sorted. It was warm for late September. Then she was led to a launch to take her to her hotel on the Grand Canal, and the whole magnificent glory that is Venice burst before her eyes.

The launch cruised up the canal, past the old palaces, past the gondolas, past boats loaded with paparazzi because of George Clooney's wedding to Amal Ala-muddin, and stopped at the hotel landing stage. Charles had booked a room with a balcony overlooking the canal in the hope that Agatha would have a place to smoke, but the window only opened a few inches.

She had heard the Piazza San Marco was near the

hotel, so after she had unpacked and put on a summer dress, she walked out of the back of the hotel, through several alleys, over a bridge, through a shopping area and arrived at the square. She found a table at Florian's in the sun, ordered a gin and tonic and felt as if she were coming alive again. She wished Charles had come with her. They had been on holiday together before. But she was only in Venice for four days—Charles's generosity having limits—before getting the train back. The orchestra was playing old-fashioned favourites like "La Paloma," the tourists came and went and Agatha could feel every tensed up muscle in her body beginning to ease.

She returned slowly to her room, suddenly tired, and went to bed, plunging down into a deep healing sleep.

Charles was trying to settle down in his study to read a detective story, but he was distracted by Gustav who, overcome with gratitude by his present of a motorbike, had decided to take on extra work, which meant clearing the bookcase and dusting the books.

"Oh, leave it alone!" complained Charles. "I want some peace. Sod off on your damned bike somewhere."

Gustav sulkily jammed the books back on the shelves, and as he did so, a small, shiny square black object fell

273

onto the floor. "This yours, sir?" he asked, handing it to Charles.

Charles stared at it in horror. "It's a tape recorder. Who put it there?"

"Blessed if I know," said Gustav.

"But who could get into the house?"

"Don't let anyone. Oh, except at the fete. Some old lady wanted the loo."

Shocked to the core, Charles told Gustav to phone the police and set off for Gatwick airport.

On the last day of her visit, Agatha felt tired, "touristed-out" as she thought of it, having diligently visited all the sites up and down the canal. She had found that smoking was allowed in an open-air bar on a platform overlooking the canal.

It was late in the evening. The only other customer was a man in a panama hat, sitting by the rail of the bar. He turned and nodded to Agatha and smiled. Agatha, still on the alert, as if by some chance Anthony had followed her to Venice, stiffened and then relaxed and smiled back. He had a white beard, neatly trimmed and bright blue eyes. He was wearing a white linen suit over a striped shirt and silk tie and his build was medium, without the stockiness and burliness of Anthony.

The water flowed by. A late gondolier with a cargo

of four tourists sailed past. Because of the strong cur-
rent, the gondolas moved fast down the canal and then
had to labour back up. Agatha had expected the canal
to smell, but the only odour was from the cigar that the
man in the panama hat had just lit. He rose and went
to the rail at the edge of the canal. "Well, I'm blessed!"
he exclaimed. "Look at that!"

Agatha joined him at the rail. "What? Where?"

"It must be my eyesight," he said ruefully. "I'll swear
I saw some fool swimming in the canal."

Agatha shrugged and sat back down and sipped
her brandy. She began to feel a lethargy creeping over
her body and decided it was time to go to bed. That
was when she found she could not move. She opened
her mouth to scream but no sound came out.

The man in the panama hat came down and sat next
to her.

"It's a wonder what plastic surgery, contact lenses, a
beard and a strict diet can do," he said. The only part
of Agatha still working was her brain. What had
happened to her famous intuition? This was Anthony
Tweedy and he was going to kill her.

"I put a drug in your drink," he said. "It paralyses
you. I want to see you suffer before I shove an overdose
of heroin into you, you interfering horrible woman. Yes.
I went to see Jill Davent. She seemed so easy to talk to
and I wanted to tell my secret to just one person. She

tried to blackmail me! Me! It was a real pleasure to get that neck of hers and wind a scarf round it and pull it till she choked to death.

"You bothered me, although I felt sure that all the stories about your detective abilities had been wildly exaggerated. I knew who Tremund was because before I killed Jill, I watched to see who called on her and found out who they were. He met me down by the canal because I said I had the dirt on Jill, so goodbye to him. And goodbye to Bannister, Herythe and Dell. Getting bored? I'll put an end to you soon. Oh, what is it?"

"Anything more to drink?" asked the waiter.

Agatha tried to signal something to him but even her eyeballs seemed frozen.

"No, we're fine." Anthony put his hand over Agatha's.

The waiter left them and went to tell the other staff that the nice Englishwoman had found romance. Agatha was considered nice because she tipped generously.

Anthony stifled a yawn. "I'm tired. Let's make an end of it before I bugger off to South America and forget you ever existed."

He took a syringe out of his pocket. God, thought Agatha, get me out of this and I'll give up smoking.

Anthony pulled Agatha's limp arm towards him. "Nice bare arms. Makes it easy."

At that moment, Charles, standing at the entrance to the bar, seized a champagne bottle from the drinks trolley and threw it with all the skill he had learnt playing village cricket with deadly accuracy. It struck Anthony on the head and he collapsed like a stone.

Horrified staff clustered in the doorway. "Ambulance!" yelled Charles. "Police!"

He gathered Agatha in his arms. "What has he done to you? Can't you speak? Is that Anthony with a face change?"

He waited in agony until a police launch roared up to the landing stage, closely followed by the ambulance launch. Charles insisted on going to the hospital with Agatha and said he would make his statement there, but he was sure the man he had struck down was the murderer, Anthony Tweedy, wanted by Interpol.

Charles was relieved to find out at the hospital that Agatha had a strong pulse. The doctors said they would not know exactly what drug had been given her until they did tests. But he was puzzled when the police told him they had not been alerted to any danger to Agatha. Surely, before he had rushed to the airport, he had told Gustav to phone the police.

Anthony Tweedy had suffered a severe concussion but was going to live. He had been travelling under a fake passport, but his real passport had been found amongst his luggage, although the police were waiting for the results of DNA tests to make absolutely sure of his identity.

Anthony recovered consciousness but continued to fake being unconscious. He waited until a nurse came to give him a sponge bath and a policeman unlocked the padded chain that held him to the bed. Through half-closed eyes he saw that the policeman had retreated to his post outside the door. Then he was in luck. Another nurse popped her head round the door and shouted that George Clooney and his wife were coming down the canal in a launch.

The nurse fled. Anthony eased himself up. There was a trolley of drugs over by the wall. With a superhuman effort, he made it out of bed. On the trolley, he found a syringe and bottles of morphine. He injected himself with an overdose and slowly collapsed onto the floor and died as the cheers from the crowds outside, watching George Clooney's launch, sounded in his ears.

Agatha was interviewed over the next few days by Wilkes and Bill Wong, who had flown out, and several hard-faced men from Interpol, along with Italian detectives, going over everything again and again until she felt she could scream. The paralysing drug that had been injected into her had such a long and complicated name, she could never remember it. She welcomed the news of Tweedy's death with relief. Agatha felt that, if he had lived, she would never have been free of the fear of him because she was sure he would have found some way to escape.

At last she was able to leave the hospital. She emerged into a strangely empty Venice compared to the last time she had seen the Grand Canal. George Clooney had left, taking with him all the world's press and all the tourists who had come to watch the show.

Charles had suggested one more night at the hotel, having cheerfully moved into Agatha's room because it had twin beds and he felt he had spent enough money on her. Using her insurance, he had cancelled her journey on the train back and booked flights home for them instead.

While Agatha and Charles sat in the bar on the last evening, Charles looked at her serene face and for once did not regret a penny he had spent on her. The old Agatha was back. Later, he thought of joining her in her bed, but resisted, feeling that a grateful Agatha might let him, and he didn't want that, although he wondered why he was suddenly developing a conscience. Agatha had asked him why he had not called the police before leaving for the airport. Charles had told her that he had asked Gustav to phone. "Better sack him," said Agatha. "He obviously didn't phone and could have got me murdered."

Back home in Carsely, Agatha felt rejuvenated and that nothing could ever upset her again. That was until Mrs. Bloxby called on her after the Sunday service to see how she was getting on and hear all about her adventures. Agatha dutifully recounted everything that had happened, but felt she had told her tale to the police so many times that her own voice sounded in her ears as if it were coming from an echo chamber.

"I still would have liked to get Gwen Simple for something," she said.

"Oh," said Mrs. Bloxby reluctantly, "you did miss the wedding."

"What wedding?"

"Mrs. Simple and Mark Dretter were married in Carsely church. They are honeymooning in Dubai."

"So all he was doing was cosying up to me to report back to that conniving bitch!"

"Mrs. Raisin!"

"Well," said Agatha huffily, "he was."

After the vicar's wife had left, Agatha sat and fretted. Gwen had not only got off scot-free, she had nailed the prize of a husband. There must be something on her.

What about Jenny Harcourt's desk at Sunnydale? Could there be something else in there?

Motivated by jealousy, Agatha set out for Sunnydale. Once more, she introduced herself as Jenny's cousin. "Mrs. Harcourt is at lunch," said a nurse. "If you would care to wait?"

"If I could please wait in her room?"

"Very well."

"It's all right," said Agatha. "I know where it is."

She ran lightly up the stairs in a new pair of flat shoes. She had not promised God not to wear high heels again although she had promised to give up smoking and so far had superstitiously kept to that promise.

Agatha opened the secret drawer in the desk. There was a magpie assortment of things from lipsticks to cheap jewellery. She was about to give up when she saw a square envelope stuck against the front flap of the drawer. She pulled it out and opened it. It was a CD. She thrust it into her handbag, just as a nurse ushered Jenny into the room.

"There you are again, dear!" cried Jenny.

"I brought you something," said Agatha, handing over a box of chocolates.

"How kind. Jenny adores chocolates. And Belgian, too!"

Her eyes fastened greedily on Agatha's handbag.

Agatha immediately zipped it up. She was anxious to escape. "I'm sorry I've got to rush, Jenny, but I didn't know you would be at lunch and I've got another appointment."

"No matter, dear. *Bargain Hunt* is about to come on the telly. Run along."

Once back in her car, Agatha was overwhelmed by a craving for a cigarette. "Sorry God," she muttered. Before driving off, she searched in the pocket of her linen skirt for her cigarette packet, which she carried around just in case she weakened. She looked back up at the building. Where she guessed Jenny's room was, the window was open and a thin trail of blue smoke was wafting out into the air.

Back in her cottage, Agatha put the CD in the player and then crouched forward in excitement. It was a recording of Jill's therapy sessions. There was Victoria confessing to drowning the dog, Doris complaining about her shoulders, Anthony Tweedy, not exactly confessing, but giving a long diatribe about how he had hated his "brother" and his fears that the fire might prove not to be accidental. Agatha only half listened to the next few sessions and then stiffened as Gwen Simple's voice began to sound. In increasing disappointment, she heard Gwen complaining about her son and wondering how on earth he could have done something so horrible without her knowledge. Nothing incriminating at all.

"I can't even give it to the police," Agatha said to her cats. "I can't have some of these poor people's sad little secrets exposed."

Although the Indian summer still seemed to stretch on forever, Doris Simpson had set a fire in the living room. Agatha lit it, waiting until there was a blaze and threw the disk onto it.

That evening, she put a cottage pie in the microwave, and then, when it was ready, picked at it, before giving up and throwing the remains on the smouldering fire.

Again, she was assailed by a terrible craving for nicotine. She hurried up to the pub. A damp breeze had sprung up. The evening sky was covered in thick black clouds. Far away came rumbles of thunder as if giants in the heavens were moving furniture.

She hurried up to the pub where she bought a packet of cigarettes, a glass of wine and a ham sandwich and walked through the pub towards the garden, getting rather sour nods by way of greeting. The villagers were beginning to think that Agatha Raisin's dangerous presence in the village was affecting house prices.

Agatha ate her sandwich and then opened the packet of cigarettes, extracted one, lit it and gratefully inhaled. There was a great flash of forked lightning, which stabbed down, missing her by inches.

She threw her cigarette away and fled back through the pub and down to her cottage through a burst of torrential rain.

"Coincidence," she muttered savagely, as she changed into dry clothes.

At the same time, Mrs. Bloxby heard the doorbell ring. "If it's that Raisin woman again, tell her to get knotted," shouted the vicar.

Mrs. Bloxby opened the door. A tall man stood on the doorstep, his face shaded by a large umbrella. "I'm new to the village," he said. "My name is Gerald Devere."

"Come in out of the rain," urged the vicar's wife. "Welcome to Carsely. Leave your coat on the stand there and let me have your umbrella. Come near the fire. Such a nasty evening. Sherry?"

"Yes, please."

Mrs. Bloxby returned, carrying a tray with the sherry decanter and two glasses. She paused for a moment in the doorway and studied her visitor. He had an interesting mobile face with a thin nose, fine grey eyes, and odd black brows that slanted upwards under a thick head of black hair with only a few threads of grey. He looked athletic, his slim body clothed in a well-tailored charcoal grey suit.

When the drinks were poured, Gerald leaned back in his chair with a sigh of satisfaction. "This is nice."

"Which cottage have you taken?" asked Mrs. Bloxby.

"Poor Mr. Dell's."

"Are you a relative?"

"No, I bought it from his niece. I've lived in London all my life and thought I would like to bury myself in the country. I'm retired."

"You look too young to retire," commented Mrs. Bloxby, guessing he must be in his middle fifties.

"I was a detective with the Metropolitan Police Force at Scotland Yard. I came into a good inheritance. I'd become weary of crime. I may have chosen the wrong village."

"Oh, we're all quiet and peaceful now." Here's someone for Mrs. Raisin, she thought. Gerald had an attractive, husky voice.

"Tell me about yourself," he said. "I should think you must have such a hardworking life."

Mrs. Bloxby blinked in amazement. Apart from Agatha, no one else ever seemed interested in her days.

"It's all the usual stuff," she said.

He grinned. "I know, therapist, mother's help, fetes,

disputes, and all exhausting and no thanks. Should I say hullo to your husband?"

"He's writing a sermon. I'll ask him."

She went along to her husband's study and told him about their visitor. "Can you cope, dear?" he asked. "I'm awfully busy."

On the road back, she popped into the bathroom and stared at her face in the mirror. Her brown hair with its streaks of grey was screwed up on top of her head. She loosened it and brushed it down before going back to join him.

They sat and talked for an hour while outside the storm rolled away. Mrs. Bloxby felt like a girl again.

After he had left, the phone rang. It was Agatha. "I hear there is some newcomer to the village," she said.

If I tell her, thought the vicar's wife, she'll be right round there, made up to the nines.

To her horror, she heard herself impulsively lying. "I wonder who that can be?" she said, blushing as she said it.

Agatha heard all about the newcomer from Phil Marshall in the office the next morning, but was not pleased to hear that a detective, however retired, had landed in her village. As far as Agatha was concerned, she was the only detective that mattered.

"There's one thing that bothers me still," she said. "I would like to know who inherits the Tweedy estate. I mean, there's madness in that family and I would like to be assured that there is not some relative of theirs going to call on me with an ax. Patrick, can you find out?"

She almost forgot about it until later in the day when Patrick said, "You're out of touch with what is going on in that village of yours. An elderly fourth cousin inherits and has been round to look at the Tweedy house. She's called Miss Delphinium Farrington."

"If the weird Tweedys went so far as to leave everything to her, then it stands to reason she must be as weird as they were. I thought people couldn't benefit from a crime."

"They can if they didn't commit it, or so I believe," said Patrick. "Although I think the insurance company will want their money back."

"You know," said Agatha, "when I had a dream of moving to a Cotswold village, I envisaged placid rosy-cheeked villagers whose families had been around for generations, not a series of murderous incomers."

"The old village families have all been priced out of their villages," said Phil.

"Well, they shouldn't have sold their properties," said Agatha ruthlessly.

At the end of another week, Agatha had decided to take the whole week-end off. She also wondered where Charles was, but put off trying to phone him. She wondered if he had fired Gustav.

Gustav was the main reason that Charles had not contacted Agatha. The trouble was, he thought, that no one had a staff of servants anymore and Gustav did so much. Gustav swore blind that he had called the police and had even written down the name of the policeman he had spoken to. When he finally questioned Bill Wong, Charles found to his relief that Gustav *had* phoned, but to Mircester headquarters instead of dialling 999, and the new copper who had taken the call had mistaken Gustav's Swiss accent for that of an East European babbling about tape recorders and so had not bothered to report it.

He called at Agatha's cottage, and finding her not at home, decided to visit Mrs. Bloxby instead.

He found Agatha, Mrs. Bloxby and a tall man who was introduced as Gerald Devere sitting in the vicarage garden. Agatha, he noticed, was wearing full war paint and was surrounded by a cloud of heavy French perfume. Oh, dear, thought Charles. Here comes obsession number 102.

Then his curious eyes fastened on the vicar's wife. He had never seen her wear her hair down before and she also had pink lipstick on. Surely not!

"Agatha!" said Charles sharply. "I hate to break up the party but I must talk to you in private."

"We're all friends here," said Agatha, flashing a coquettish look from under heavily mascaraed eyelashes at Gerald.

"It's private and very urgent," said Charles.

Agatha sulkily agreed to leave with him.

"We'll go to the pub," said Charles. "I need a stiff drink."

"Let's just hope you've got your wallet," said Agatha sourly.

Once they were seated in the pub, Charles said, "Back off from Gerald, Aggie."

"Why on earth . . . ?"

"Mrs. Bloxby's got a crush on him."

"Never! She wouldn't. She's a saint!"

"She's human and leads a dreary life. She won't do anything about it, Aggie, but let her have one little dream and stop jumping all over it with your stilettos."

Agatha opened her mouth to make a sharp retort and then closed it again. She remembered that pink lipstick and the hair brushed down on the shoulders. Also, the vicar's wife had been wearing a smart green wool dress Agatha had not seen before.

But Gerald was so, well, *marriageable*. And Mrs. Bloxby *was* married. Therefore, surely if Agatha lured

Gerald away she would be saving her friend from disaster, pain and a possible broken marriage.

Charles studied the emotions flitting across Agatha's face. "You like me as a friend, don't you, Agatha?"

"Of course," she said. "You've saved my life."

"I don't want your gratitude," snapped Charles. "I just don't want you to do anything to ruin our friendship. And competing with Mrs. Bloxby is just not on."

"Oh, all right," said Agatha. "If you say so."

It was evening before Charles took himself off. Church in the morning, thought Agatha happily. Gerald's bound to be in church.

The real autumn had come at last when Agatha set off for the church, more soberly dressed and made-up than usual, just in case Charles should take it into his head to check up on her to see if she was following orders. Throughout the service, Agatha spent the time arguing with the God she only believed in in times of stress about her smoking habit and how it was only a little sin. She could not spot Mrs. Bloxby but she did recognise Gerald's tall figure.

Agatha stood outside and waited for him to emerge. He came out at last and beside him was a new Mrs. Bloxby with her hair tinted rich brown and worn in a coronet on top of her head. *And* she was wearing a glamorous white fun fur. Her gentle face was delicately made up.

As she approached them, Gerald said, "See you later, Margaret," nodded to Agatha and hurried off.

Other parishioners came up to talk to the vicar's wife and Agatha rushed off, her mind racing. Yes, she really would be doing Mrs. Bloxby a favour if she could lure Gerald away.

She remembered Doris had baked her a lemon drizzle cake, which she had stored in her kitchen freezer. She would take that to Gerald as a welcome to the village. She took it out of the freezer. It was covered in frost and as hard as a brick. She shoved it in the microwave but forgot to turn the dial to defrost. When she took it out, it appeared to have half melted over the plate. Determined not to let this setback stop her, she firmly wrapped the hot melting mess in cling film, put it in a bag and headed up to Gerald's villa. He answered the door and stood looking down at her. "Mrs. Raisin?"

"I told you to call me Agatha," said Agatha with what she hoped was a winning smile. "I've brought you a cake."

"Dear me. What a hospitable lot you ladies are! I have so many cakes. Are you sure you don't want to keep it?"

"No, please take it."

"You must excuse me. I am in the middle of an important phone call. Another time?"

He took the bag from her, went in and shut the door.

Snakes and bastards, thought Agatha furiously. I don't believe that phone call. What if he's got Mrs. Bloxby in there?

She moved a little away, but then burning curiosity overtook her. She walked quietly up the side of his villa, hoping to be able to peer in the French windows that overlooked the garden at the back.

She moved silently up to the windows. She could see nothing in the windows except her own reflection. Agatha pressed her face against the glass and cupped her hands.

"What on earth do you think you are doing?" came a harsh voice from behind her.

Agatha jumped nervously and turned round to find Gerald staring down at her. "I was in the potting shed and saw you snooping."

"I was leaving and I thought I saw some stranger going up the side of your house. I thought I had better check," said Agatha desperately.

"As you can see, I am all right. Goodbye." He turned on his heel and strode back to the potting shed.

Agatha trailed miserably off. If only she had decided to work at the week-end. Now she was left with a long empty day to think about how silly she had been.

The phone was ringing when she let herself into her cottage. She rushed to answer it. It was Mrs. Bloxby. "Have you got time to drop up here?" she asked. "I want to consult you about something."

"Sure," said Agatha dismally. "Be right with you."

What if Gerald told her about me snooping? thought Agatha. Or how will I handle it if she confesses to being in love with him?

At the vicarage, Mrs. Bloxby ushered Agatha into the drawing room. Agatha was too nervous to accept any offer of refreshment, saying, "What is it?"

"It's the allotments."

"Those strips of land outside the village?" said Agatha, bewildered.

"Yes. The problem is that they were owned by a trust which has lapsed and the land now belongs to Lord Bellington. He wants to sell the land to a developer and put a housing estate on it."

"If he has the legal right to do so, then I cannot see what anyone can do about it," said Agatha.

"But I wondered if you could engineer some publicity and start up a petition," said Mrs. Bloxby.

Agatha half-closed her eyes as a horrible memory of being nearly buried alive in an allotment flooded back into her mind.

She stood up abruptly.

"I'm sorry, but quite frankly it will be a cold day in

hell before I have anything to do with allotments again."

Mrs. Bloxby stared in dismay as Agatha went out of the vicarage and off into the village.

Agatha Raisin was not to know how wrong she was and how those wretched village allotments would lead to murder.